Kazan

Kazan

James Oliver Curwood

MINT EDITIONS

Kazan was first published in 1914.

This edition published by Mint Editions 2021.

ISBN 9781513280738 | E-ISBN 9781513285757

Published by Mint Editions®

 MINT
EDITIONS
minteditionbooks.com

Publishing Director: Jennifer Newens
Design & Production: Rachel Lopez Metzger
Project Manager: Micaela Clark
Typesetting: Westchester Publishing Services

Contents

I. The Miracle   7

II. Into the North   11

III. McCready Pays the Debt   16

IV. Free from Bonds   22

V. The Fight in the Snow   32

VI. Joan   38

VII. Out of the Blizzard   47

VIII. The Great Change   53

IX. The Tragedy on Sun Rock   58

X. The Days of Fire   65

XI. Always Two by Two   71

XII. The Red Death   79

XIII. The Trail of Hunger   86

XIV. The Right of Fang   92

XV. A Fight Under the Stars   95

XVI. The Call   99

XVII. His Son   106

XVIII. The Education of Ba-ree   111

XIX. The Usurpers   117

XX. A Feud in the Wilderness   122

XXI. A Shot on the Sand-Bar   131

XXII. Sandy's Method   136

XXIII. Professor McGill   142

XXIV. Alone in Darkness   146

XXV. The Last of McTrigger   150

XXVI. An Empty World   155

XXVII. The Call of Sun Rock   158

I

The Miracle

Kazan lay mute and motionless, his gray nose between his forepaws, his eyes half closed. A rock could have appeared scarcely less lifeless than he; not a muscle twitched; not a hair moved; not an eyelid quivered. Yet every drop of the wild blood in his splendid body was racing in a ferment of excitement that Kazan had never before experienced; every nerve and fiber of his wonderful muscles was tense as steel wire. Quarter-strain wolf, three-quarters "husky," he had lived the four years of his life in the wilderness. He had felt the pangs of starvation. He knew what it meant to freeze. He had listened to the wailing winds of the long Arctic night over the barrens. He had heard the thunder of the torrent and the cataract, and had cowered under the mighty crash of the storm. His throat and sides were scarred by battle, and his eyes were red with the blister of the snows. He was called Kazan, the Wild Dog, because he was a giant among his kind and as fearless, even, as the men who drove him through the perils of a frozen world.

He had never known fear—until now. He had never felt in him before the desire to *run*—not even on that terrible day in the forest when he had fought and killed the big gray lynx. He did not know what it was that frightened him, but he knew that he was in another world, and that many things in it startled and alarmed him. It was his first glimpse of civilization. He wished that his master would come back into the strange room where he had left him. It was a room filled with hideous things. There were great human faces on the wall, but they did not move or speak, but stared at him in a way he had never seen people look before. He remembered having looked on a master who lay very quiet and very cold in the snow, and he had sat back on his haunches and wailed forth the death song; but these people on the walls looked alive, and yet seemed dead.

Suddenly Kazan lifted his ears a little. He heard steps, then low voices. One of them was his master's voice. But the other—it sent a little tremor through him! Once, so long ago that it must have been in his puppyhood days, he seemed to have had a dream of a laugh that was like the girl's laugh—a laugh that was all at once filled with a wonderful happiness, the thrill of a wonderful love, and a sweetness that made Kazan lift his head as they came in. He looked straight at them, his red eyes gleaming. At once he knew that she must be dear to his master, for his master's arm was about her. In the glow of the light he saw that her hair was very bright, and that there was the color of the crimson *bakneesh* vine in her face and the blue of the *bakneesh* flower in her shining eyes. Suddenly she saw him, and with a little cry darted toward him.

"Stop!" shouted the man. "He's dangerous! Kazan—"

She was on her knees beside him, all fluffy and sweet and beautiful, her eyes shining wonderfully, her hands about to touch him. Should he cringe back? Should he snap? Was she one of the things on the wall, and his enemy? Should he leap at her white throat? He saw the man running forward, pale as death. Then her hand fell upon his head and the touch sent a thrill through him that quivered in every nerve of his body. With both hands she turned up his head. Her face was very close, and he heard her say, almost sobbingly:

"And you are Kazan—dear old Kazan, my Kazan, my hero dog—who brought him home to me when all the others had died! My Kazan—my hero!"

And then, miracle of miracles, her face was crushed down against him, and he felt her sweet warm touch.

In those moments Kazan did not move. He scarcely breathed. It seemed a long time before the girl lifted her face from him. And when she did, there were tears in her blue eyes, and the man was standing above them, his hands gripped tight, his jaws set.

"I never knew him to let any one touch him—with their naked hand," he said in a tense wondering voice. "Move back quietly, Isobel. Good heaven—look at that!"

Kazan whined softly, his bloodshot eyes on the girl's face. He wanted to feel her hand again; he wanted to touch her face. Would they beat him with a club, he wondered, if he *dared*! He meant no harm now. He would kill for her. He cringed toward her, inch by inch, his eyes never faltering. He heard what the man said—"Good heaven! Look at that!"—and he shuddered. But no blow fell to drive him back. His cold muzzle touched her filmy dress, and she looked at him, without moving, her wet eyes blazing like stars.

"See!" she whispered. "See!"

Half an inch more—an inch, two inches, and he gave his big gray body a hunch toward her. Now his muzzle traveled slowly upward—

over her foot, to her lap, and at last touched the warm little hand that lay there. His eyes were still on her face: he saw a queer throbbing in her bare white throat, and then a trembling of her lips as she looked up at the man with a wonderful look. He, too, knelt down beside them, and put his arm about the girl again, and patted the dog on his head. Kazan did not like the man's touch. He mistrusted it, as nature had taught him to mistrust the touch of all men's hands, but he permitted it because he saw that it in some way pleased the girl.

"Kazan, old boy, you wouldn't hurt her, would you?" said his master softly. "We both love her, don't we, boy? Can't help it, can we? And she's ours, Kazan, all *ours*! She belongs to you and to me, and we're going to take care of her all our lives, and if we ever have to we'll fight for her like hell—won't we? Eh, Kazan, old boy?"

For a long time after they left him where he was lying on the rug, Kazan's eyes did not leave the girl. He watched and listened—and all the time there grew more and more in him the craving to creep up to them and touch the girl's hand, or her dress, or her foot. After a time his master said something, and with a little laugh the girl jumped up and ran to a big, square, shining thing that stood crosswise in a corner, and which had a row of white teeth longer than his own body. He had wondered what those teeth were for. The girl's fingers touched them now, and all the whispering of winds that he had ever heard, all the music of the waterfalls and the rapids and the trilling of birds in springtime, could not equal the sounds they made. It was his first music. For a moment it startled and frightened him, and then he felt the fright pass away and a strange tingling in his body. He wanted to sit back on his haunches and howl, as he had howled at the billion stars in the skies on cold winter nights. But something kept him from doing that. It was the girl. Slowly he began slinking toward her. He felt the eyes of the man upon him, and stopped. Then a little more—inches at a time, with his throat and jaw straight out along the floor! He was half-way to her—half-way across the room—when the wonderful sounds grew very soft and very low

"Go on!" he heard the man urge in a low quick voice. "Go on! Don't stop!"

The girl turned her head, saw Kazan cringing there on the floor, and continued to play. The man was still looking, but his eyes could not keep Kazan back now. He went nearer, still nearer, until at last his outreaching muzzle touched her dress where it lay piled on the floor.

And then—he lay trembling, for she had begun to sing. He had heard a Cree woman crooning in front of her tepee; he had heard the wild chant of the caribou song—but he had never heard anything like this wonderful sweetness that fell from the lips of the girl. He forgot his master's presence now. Quietly, cringingly, so that she would not know, he lifted his head. He saw her looking at him; there was something in her wonderful eyes that gave him confidence, and he laid his head in her lap. For the second time he felt the touch of a woman's hand, and he closed his eyes with a long sighing breath. The music stopped. There came a little fluttering sound above him, like a laugh and a sob in one. He heard his master cough.

"I've always loved the old rascal—but I never thought he'd do that," he said; and his voice sounded queer to Kazan.

II

Into the North

Wonderful days followed for Kazan. He missed the forests and deep snows. He missed the daily strife of keeping his teammates in trace, the yapping at his heels, the straight long pull over the open spaces and the barrens. He missed the "Koosh—koosh—Hooyah!" of the driver, the spiteful snap of his twenty-foot caribou-gut whip, and that yelping and straining behind him that told him he had his followers in line. But something had come to take the place of that which he missed. It was in the room, in the air all about him, even when the girl or his master was not near. Wherever she had been, he found the presence of that strange thing that took away his loneliness. It was the woman scent, and sometimes it made him whine softly when the girl herself was actually with him. He was not lonely, nights, when he should have been out howling at the stars. He was not lonely, because one night he prowled about until he found a certain door, and when the girl opened that door in the morning she found him curled up tight against it. She had reached down and hugged him, the thick smother of her long hair falling all over him in a delightful perfume; thereafter she placed a rug before the door for him to sleep on. All through the long nights he knew that she was just beyond the door, and he was content. Each day he thought less and less of the wild places, and more of her.

Then there came the beginning of the change. There was a strange hurry and excitement around him, and the girl paid less attention to him. He grew uneasy. He sniffed the change in the air, and he began to study his master's face. Then there came the morning, very early, when the babiche collar and the iron chain were fastened to him again. Not until he had followed his master out through the door and into the street did he begin to understand. They were sending him away! He sat suddenly back on his haunches and refused to budge.

"Come, Kazan," coaxed the man. "Come on, boy."

He hung back and showed his white fangs. He expected the lash of a whip or the blow of a club, but neither came. His master laughed and took him back to the house. When they left it again, the girl was with them and walked with her hand touching his head. It was she who persuaded him to leap up through a big dark hole into the still darker interior of a car, and it was she who lured him to the darkest corner of all, where his master fastened his chain. Then they went out, laughing like two children. For hours after that, Kazan lay still and tense, listening to the queer rumble of wheels under him. Several times those wheels stopped, and he heard voices outside. At last he was sure that he heard a familiar voice, and he strained at his chain and whined. The closed door slid back. A man with a lantern climbed in, followed by his master. He paid no attention to them, but glared out through the opening into the gloom of night. He almost broke loose when he leaped down upon the white snow, but when he saw no one there, he stood rigid, sniffing the air. Over him were the stars he had howled at all his life, and about him were the forests, black and silent, shutting them in like a wall. Vainly he sought for that one scent that was missing, and Thorpe heard the low note of grief in his shaggy throat. He took the lantern and held it above his head, at the same time loosening his hold on the leash. At that signal there came a voice from out of the night. It came from behind them, and Kazan whirled so suddenly that the loosely held chain slipped from the man's hand. He saw the glow of other lanterns. And then, once more, the voice—

"Kaa-aa-zan!"

He was off like a bolt. Thorpe laughed to himself as he followed.

"The old pirate!" he chuckled.

When he came to the lantern-lighted space back of the caboose, Thorpe found Kazan crouching down at a woman's feet. It was Thorpe's wife. She smiled triumphantly at him as he came up out of the gloom.

"You've won!" he laughed, not unhappily. "I'd have wagered my last dollar he wouldn't do that for any voice on earth. You've won! Kazan, you brute, I've lost you!"

His face suddenly sobered as Isobel stooped to pick up the end of the chain.

"He's yours, Issy," he added quickly, "but you must let me care for him until—we *know*. Give me the chain. I won't trust him even now. He's a wolf. I've seen him take an Indian's hand off at a single snap. I've seen him tear out another dog's jugular in one leap. He's an outlaw—a bad dog—in spite of the fact that he hung to me like a hero and brought me out alive. I can't trust him. Give me the chain—"

He did not finish. With the snarl of a wild beast Kazan had leaped

JAMES OLIVER CURWOOD

ps drew up and bared his long

a sudden cry of warning, Thorpe dr

elt.

o attention to him. Another form had

ght, and stood now in the circle of illuminatio

ns. It was McCready, who was to accompany Thorp

young wife back to the Red River camp, where Thorpe was in

of the building of the new Trans-continental. The man was st

powerfully built and clean shaven. His jaw was so square that it

brutal, and there was a glow in his eyes that was almost like the passr

in Kazan's as he looked at Isobel.

Her red and white stocking-cap had slipped free of her head and was hanging over her shoulder. The dull blaze of the lanterns shone in the warm glow of her hair. Her cheeks were flushed, and her eyes, suddenly turned to him, were as blue as the bluest *bakneesh* flower and glowed like diamonds. McCready shifted his gaze, and instantly her hand fell on Kazan's head. For the first time the dog did not seem to feel her touch. He still snarled at McCready, the rumbling menace in his throat growing deeper. Thorpe's wife tugged at the chain.

"Down, Kazan—down!" she commanded.

At the sound of her voice he relaxed.

"Down!" she repeated, and her free hand fell on his head again. He slunk to her feet. But his lips were still drawn back. Thorpe was watching him. He wondered at the deadly venom that shot from the wolfish eyes, and looked at McCready. The big guide had uncoiled his long dog-whip. A strange look had come into his face. He was staring hard at Kazan. Suddenly he leaned forward, with both hands on his knees, and for a tense moment or two he seemed to forget that Isobel Thorpe's wonderful blue eyes were looking at him.

"Hoo-koosh, Pedro—*charge!*"

That one word—*charge*—was taught only to the dogs in the service of the Northwest Mounted Police. Kazan did not move. McCready straightened, and quick as a shot sent the long lash of his whip curling out into the night with a crack like a pistol report.

"Charge, Pedro—*charge!*"

The rumble in Kazan's throat deepened to a snarling growl, but not a muscle of his body moved. McCready turned to Thorpe.

"I could have sworn that I knew that dog," he said. "If it's Pedro, he's *bad!*"

king the chain. Only the girl saw the look th
to McCready's face. It made her shiver. A few m
he train had first stopped at Les Pas, she had offered
nan and she had seen the same thing then. But even as she
she recalled the many things her husband had told her of the
ple. She had grown to love them, to admire their big rough
d and loyal hearts, before he had brought her among them; and
ly she smiled at McCready, struggling to overcome that thrill of
and dislike.

He doesn't like you," she laughed at him softly. "Won't you make
iends with him?"

She drew Kazan toward him, with Thorpe holding the end of the chain. McCready came to her side as she bent over the dog. His back was to Thorpe as he hunched down. Isobel's bowed head was within a foot of his face. He could see the glow in her cheek and the pouting curve of her mouth as she quieted the low rumbling in Kazan's throat. Thorpe stood ready to pull back on the chain, but for a moment McCready was between him and his wife, and he could not see McCready's face. The man's eyes were not on Kazan. He was staring at the girl.

"You're brave," he said. "I don't dare do that. He would take off my hand!"

He took the lantern from Thorpe and led the way to a narrow snow-path branching off, from the track. Hidden back in the thick spruce was the camp that Thorpe had left a fortnight before. There were two tents there now in place of the one that he and his guide had used. A big fire was burning in front of them. Close to the fire was a long sledge, and fastened to trees just within the outer circle of firelight Kazan saw the shadowy forms and gleaming eyes of his team-mates. He stood stiff and motionless while Thorpe fastened him to a sledge. Once more he was back in his forests—and in command. His mistress was laughing and clapping her hands delightedly in the excitement of the strange and wonderful life of which she had now become a part. Thorpe had thrown back the flap of their tent, and she was entering ahead of him. She did not look back. She spoke no word to him. He whined, and turned his red eyes on McCready.

In the tent Thorpe was saying:

"I'm sorry old Jackpine wouldn't go back with us, Issy. He drove me down, but for love or money I couldn't get him to return. He's a Mission Indian, and I'd give a month's salary to have you see him handle the dogs. I'm not sure about this man McCready. He's a queer chap, the Company's agent here tells me, and knows the woods like a book. But dogs don't like a stranger. Kazan isn't going to take to him worth a cent!"

Kazan heard the girl's voice, and stood rigid and motionless listening to it. He did not hear or see McCready when he came up stealthily behind him. The man's voice came as suddenly as a shot at his heels.

"*Pedro!*"

In an instant Kazan cringed as if touched by a lash.

"Got you that time—didn't I, you old devil!" whispered McCready, his face strangely pale in the firelight. "Changed your name, eh? But I *got* you—didn't I?"

III

McCready Pays the Debt

For a long time after he had uttered those words McCready sat in silence beside the fire. Only for a moment or two at a time did his eyes leave Kazan. After a little, when he was sure that Thorpe and Isobel had retired for the night, he went into his own tent and returned with a flask of whisky. During the next half-hour he drank frequently. Then he went over and sat on the end of the sledge, just beyond the reach of Kazan's chain.

"Got you, didn't I?" he repeated, the effect of the liquor beginning to show in the glitter of his eyes. "Wonder who changed your name, Pedro. And how the devil did *he* come by you? Ho, ho, if you could only talk—"

They heard Thorpe's voice inside the tent. It was followed by a low girlish peal of laughter, and McCready jerked himself erect. His face blazed suddenly red, and he rose to his feet, dropping the flask in his coat pocket. Walking around the fire, he tiptoed cautiously to the shadow of a tree close to the tent and stood there for many minutes listening. His eyes burned with a fiery madness when he returned to the sledge and Kazan. It was midnight before he went into his own tent.

In the warmth of the fire, Kazan's eyes slowly closed. He slumbered uneasily, and his brain was filled with troubled pictures. At times he was fighting, and his jaws snapped. At others he was straining at the end of his chain, with McCready or his mistress just out of reach. He felt the gentle touch of the girl's hand again and heard the wonderful sweetness of her voice as she sang to him and his master, and his body trembled and twitched with the thrills that had filled him that night. And then the picture changed. He was running at the head of a splendid team— six dogs of the Royal Northwest Mounted Police—and his master was calling him Pedro! The scene shifted. They were in camp. His master was young and smooth-faced and he helped from the sledge another man whose hands were fastened in front of him by curious black rings. Again it was later—and he was lying before a great fire. His master was sitting opposite him, with his back to a tent, and as he looked, there came out of the tent the man with the black rings—only now the rings were gone and his hands were free, and in one of them he carried a heavy club. He heard the terrible blow of the club as it fell on his master's head—and the sound of it aroused him from his restless sleep.

He sprang to his feet, his spine stiffening and a snarl in his throat. The fire had died down and the camp was in the darker gloom that precedes dawn. Through that gloom Kazan saw McCready. Again he was standing close to the tent of his mistress, and he knew now that this was the man who had worn the black iron rings, and that it was he who had beaten him with whip and club for many long days after he had killed his master. McCready heard the menace in his throat and came back quickly to the fire. He began to whistle and draw the half-burned logs together, and as the fire blazed up afresh he shouted to awaken Thorp and Isobel. In a few minutes Thorpe appeared at the tent-flap and his wife followed him out. Her loose hair rippled in billows of gold about her shoulders and she sat down on the sledge, close to Kazan, and began brushing it. McCready came up behind her and fumbled among the packages on the sledge. As if by accident one of his hands buried itself for an instant in the rich tresses that flowed down her back. She did not at first feel the caressing touch of his fingers, and Thorpe's back was toward them.

Only Kazan saw the stealthy movement of the hand, the fondling clutch of the fingers in her hair, and the mad passion burning in the eyes of the man. Quicker than a lynx, the dog had leaped the length of his chain across the sledge. McCready sprang back just in time, and as Kazan reached the end of his chain he was jerked back so that his body struck sidewise against the girl. Thorpe had turned in time to see the end of the leap. He believed that Kazan had sprung at Isobel, and in his horror no word or cry escaped his lips as he dragged her from where she had half fallen over the sledge. He saw that she was not hurt, and he reached for his revolver. It was in his holster in the tent. At his feet was McCready's whip, and in the passion of the moment he seized it and sprang upon Kazan. The dog crouched in the snow. He made no move to escape or to attack. Only once in his life could he remember having received a beating like that which Thorpe inflicted upon him now. But not a whimper or a growl escaped him.

And then, suddenly, his mistress ran forward and caught the whip poised above Thorpe's head.

"Not another blow!" she cried, and something in her voice held him from striking. McCready did not hear what she said then, but a strange look came into Thorpe's eyes, and without a word he followed his wife into their tent.

"Kazan did not leap at me," she whispered, and she was trembling with a sudden excitement. Her face was deathly white. "That man was behind me," she went on, clutching her husband by the arm. "I felt him touch me—and then Kazan sprang. He wouldn't bite *me*. It's the *man*! There's something—wrong—"

She was almost sobbing, and Thorpe drew her close in his arms.

"I hadn't thought before—but it's strange," he said. "Didn't McCready say something about knowing the dog? It's possible. Perhaps he's had Kazan before and abused him in a way that the dog has not forgotten. To-morrow I'll find out. But until I know—will you promise to keep away from Kazan?"

Isobel gave the promise. When they came out from the tent Kazan lifted his great head. The stinging lash had closed one of his eyes and his mouth was dripping blood. Isobel gave a low sob, but did not go near him. Half blinded, he knew that his mistress had stopped his punishment, and he whined softly, and wagged his thick tail in the snow.

Never had he felt so miserable as through the long hard hours of the day that followed, when he broke the trail for his team-mates into the North. One of his eyes was closed and filled with stinging fire, and his body was sore from the blows of the caribou lash. But it was not physical pain that gave the sullen droop to his head and robbed his body of that keen quick alertness of the lead-dog—the commander of his mates. It was his spirit. For the first time in his life, it was broken. McCready had beaten him—long ago; his master had beaten him; and during all this day their voices were fierce and vengeful in his ears. But it was his mistress who hurt him most. She held aloof from him, always beyond they reach of his leash; and when they stopped to rest, and again in camp, she looked at him with strange and wondering eyes, and did not speak. She, too, was ready to beat him. He believed that, and so slunk away from her and crouched on his belly in the snow. With him, a broken spirit meant a broken heart, and that night he lurked in one of the deepest shadows about the camp-fire and grieved alone. None knew that it was grief—unless it was the girl. She did not move toward him. She did not speak to him. But she watched him closely—and studied him hardest when he was looking at McCready.

Later, after Thorpe and his wife had gone into their tent, it began to snow, and the effect of the snow upon McCready puzzled Kazan. The man was restless, and he drank frequently from the flask that he had used the night before. In the firelight his face grew redder and redder, and Kazan could see the strange gleam of his teeth as he gazed at the tent in which his mistress was sleeping. Again and again he went close to that tent, and listened. Twice he heard movement. The last time, it was the sound of Thorpe's deep breathing. McCready hurried back to the fire and turned his face straight up to the sky. The snow was falling so thickly that when he lowered his face he blinked and wiped his eyes. Then he went out into the gloom and bent low over the trail they had made a few hours before. It was almost obliterated by the falling snow. Another hour and there would be no trail—nothing the next day to tell whoever might pass that they had come this way. By morning it would cover everything, even the fire, if he allowed it to die down. McCready drank again, out in the darkness. Low words of an insane joy burst from his lips. His head was hot with a drunken fire. His heart beat madly, but scarcely more furiously than did Kazan's when the dog saw that McCready was returning *with a club*! The club he placed on end against a tree. Then he took a lantern from the sledge and lighted it. He approached Thorpe's tent-flap, the lantern in his hand.

"Ho, Thorpe—Thorpe!" he called.

There was no answer. He could hear Thorpe breathing. He drew the flap aside a little, and raised his voice.

"Thorpe!"

Still there was no movement inside, and he untied the flap strings and thrust in his lantern. The light flashed on Isobel's golden head, and McCready stared at it, his eyes burning like red coals, until he saw that Thorpe was awakening. Quickly he dropped the flap and rustled it from the outside.

"Ho, Thorpe!—Thorpe!" he called again.

This time Thorpe replied.

"Hello, McCready—is that you?"

McCready drew the flap back a little, and spoke in a low voice.

"Yes. Can you come out a minute? Something's happening out in the woods. Don't wake up your wife!"

He drew back and waited. A minute later Thorpe came quietly out of the tent. McCready pointed into the thick spruce.

"I'll swear there's some one nosing around the camp," he said. "I'm certain that I saw a man out there a few minutes ago, when I went for a log. It's a good night for stealing dogs. Here—you take the lantern! If I wasn't clean fooled, we'll find a trail in the snow."

He gave Thorpe the lantern and picked up the heavy club. A growl rose in Kazan's throat, but he choked it back. He wanted to snarl forth his warning, to leap at the end of his leash, but he knew that if he did that, they would return and beat him. So he lay still, trembling and shivering, and whining softly. He watched them until they disappeared—and then waited—listened. At last he heard the crunch of snow. He was not surprised to see McCready come back alone. He had expected him to return alone. For he knew what a club meant!

McCready's face was terrible now. It was like a beast's. He was hatless. Kazan slunk deeper in his shadow at the low horrible laugh that fell from his lips—for the man still held the club. In a moment he dropped that, and approached the tent. He drew back the flap and peered in. Thorpe's wife was sleeping, and as quietly as a cat he entered and hung the lantern on a nail in the tent-pole. His movement did not awaken her, and for a few moments he stood there, staring—staring.

Outside, crouching in the deep shadow, Kazan tried to fathom the meaning of these strange things that were happening. Why had his master and McCready gone out into the forest? Why had not his master returned? It was his master, and not McCready, who belonged in that tent. Then why was McCready there? He watched McCready as he entered, and suddenly the dog was on his feet, his back tense and bristling, his limbs rigid. He saw McCready's huge shadow on the canvas, and a moment later there came a strange piercing cry. In the wild terror of that cry he recognized *her* voice—and he leaped toward the tent. The leash stopped him, choking the snarl in his throat. He saw the shadows struggling now, and there came cry after cry. She was calling to his master, and with his master's name she was calling *him*!

"*Kazan—Kazan—*"

He leaped again, and was thrown upon his back. A second and a third time he sprang the length of the leash into the night, and the babiche cord about his neck cut into his flesh like a knife. He stopped for an instant, gasping for breath. The shadows were still fighting. Now they were upright! Now they were crumpling down! With a fierce snarl he flung his whole weight once more at the end of the chain. There was a snap, as the thong about his neck gave way.

In half a dozen bounds Kazan made the tent and rushed under the flap. With a snarl he was at McCready's throat. The first snap of his powerful jaws was death, but he did not know that. He knew only that his mistress was there, and that he was fighting for her. There came one choking gasping cry that ended with a terrible sob; it was McCready. The man sank from his knees upon his back, and Kazan thrust his fangs deeper into his enemy's throat; he felt the warm blood.

The dog's mistress was calling to him now. She was pulling at his shaggy neck. But he would not loose his hold—not for a long time. When he did, his mistress looked down once upon the man and covered her face with her hands. Then she sank down upon the blankets. She was very still. Her face and hands were cold, and Kazan muzzled them tenderly. Her eyes were closed. He snuggled up close against her, with his ready jaws turned toward the dead man. Why was she so still, he wondered?

A long time passed, and then she moved. Her eyes opened. Her hand touched him.

Then he heard a step outside.

It was his master, and with that old thrill of fear—fear of the club— he went swiftly to the door. Yes, there was his master in the firelight— and in his hand he held the club. He was coming slowly, almost falling at each step, and his face was red with blood. But he had *the club*! He would beat him again—beat him terribly for hurting McCready; so Kazan slipped quietly under the tent-flap and stole off into the shadows. From out the gloom of the thick spruce he looked back, and a low whine of love and grief rose and died softly in his throat. They would beat him always now—after *that*. Even *she* would beat him. They would hunt him down, and beat him when they found him.

From out of the glow of the fire he turned his wolfish head to the depths of the forest. There were no clubs or stinging lashes out in that gloom. They would never find him there.

For another moment he wavered. And then, as silently as one of the wild creatures whose blood was partly his, he stole away into the blackness of the night.

IV

Free from Bonds

There was a low moaning of the wind in the spruce-tops as Kazan slunk off into the blackness and mystery of the forest. For hours he lay near the camp, his red and blistered eyes gazing steadily at the tent wherein the terrible thing had happened a little while before.

He knew now what death was. He could tell it farther than man. He could smell it in the air. And he knew that there was death all about him, and that he was the cause of it. He lay on his belly in the deep snow and shivered, and the three-quarters of him that was dog whined in a grief-stricken way, while the quarter that was wolf still revealed itself menacingly in his fangs, and in the vengeful glare of his eyes.

Three times the man—his master—came out of the tent, and shouted loudly, "Kazan—Kazan—Kazan!"

Three times the woman came with him. In the firelight Kazan could see her shining hair streaming about her, as he had seen it in the tent, when he had leaped up and killed the other man. In her blue eyes there was the same wild terror, and her face was white as the snow. And the second and third time, she too called, "Kazan—Kazan—Kazan!"—and all that part of him that was dog, and not wolf, trembled joyously at the sound of her voice, and he almost crept in to take his beating. But fear of the club was the greater, and he held back, hour after hour, until now it was silent again in the tent, and he could no longer see their shadows, and the fire was dying down.

Cautiously he crept out from the thick gloom, working his way on his belly toward the packed sledge, and what remained of the burned logs. Beyond that sledge, hidden in the darkness of the trees, was the body of the man he had killed, covered with a blanket. Thorpe, his master, had dragged it there.

He lay down, with his nose to the warm coals and his eyes leveled between his forepaws, straight at the closed tent-flap. He meant to keep awake, to watch, to be ready to slink off into the forest at the first movement there. But a warmth was rising from out of the gray ash of the fire-bed, and his eyes closed. Twice—three times—he fought himself back into watchfulness; but the last time his eyes came only half open, and closed heavily again.

And now, in his sleep, he whined softly, and the splendid muscles of his legs and shoulders twitched, and sudden shuddering ripples ran along his tawny spine. Thorpe, who was in the tent, if he had seen him, would have known that he was dreaming. And Thorpe's wife, whose golden head lay close against his breast, and who shuddered and trembled now and then even as Kazan was doing, would have known what he was dreaming about.

In his sleep he was leaping again at the end of his chain. His jaws snapped like castanets of steel,—and the sound awakened him, and he sprang to his feet, his spine as stiff as a brush, and his snarling fangs bared like ivory knives. He had awakened just in time. There was movement in the tent. His master was awake, and if he did not escape—

He sped swiftly into the thick spruce, and paused, flat and hidden, with only his head showing from behind a tree. He knew that his master would not spare him. Three times Thorpe had beaten him for snapping at McCready. The last time he would have shot him if the girl had not saved him. And now he had torn McCready's throat. He had taken the life from him, and his master would not spare him. Even the woman could not save him.

Kazan was sorry that his master had returned, dazed and bleeding, after he had torn McCready's jugular. Then he would have had her always. She would have loved him. She did love him. And he would have followed her, and fought for her always, and died for her when the time came. But Thorpe had come in from the forest again, and Kazan had slunk away quickly—for Thorpe meant to him what all men meant to him now: the club, the whip and the strange things that spat fire and death. And now—

Thorpe had come out from the tent. It was approaching dawn, and in his hand he held a rifle. A moment later the girl came out, and her hand caught the man's arm. They looked toward the thing covered by the blanket. Then she spoke to Thorpe and he suddenly straightened and threw back his head.

"H-o-o-o-o—Kazan—Kazan—Kazan!" he called.

A shiver ran through Kazan. The man was trying to inveigle him back. He had in his hand the thing that killed.

"Kazan—Kazan—Ka-a-a-a-zan!" he shouted again.

Kazan sneaked cautiously back from the tree. He knew that distance meant nothing to the cold thing of death that Thorpe held in his hand. He turned his head once, and whined softly, and for an instant a great longing filled his reddened eyes as he saw the last of the girl.

He knew, now, that he was leaving her forever, and there was an ache in his heart that had never been there before, a pain that was not of the club or whip, of cold or hunger, but which was greater than them all, and which filled him with a desire to throw back his head and cry out his loneliness to the gray emptiness of the sky.

Back in the camp the girl's voice quivered.

"He is gone."

The man's strong voice choked a little.

"Yes, he is gone. *He knew*—and I didn't. I'd give—a year of my life—if I hadn't whipped him yesterday and last night. He won't come back."

Isobel Thorpe's hand tightened on his arm.

"He will!" she cried. "He won't leave me. He loved me, if he was savage and terrible. And he knows that I love him. He'll come back—"

"Listen!"

From deep in the forest there came a long wailing howl, filled with a plaintive sadness. It was Kazan's farewell to the woman.

After that cry Kazan sat for a long time on his haunches, sniffing the new freedom of the air, and watching the deep black pits in the forest about him, as they faded away before dawn. 'Now and then, since the day the traders had first bought him and put him into sledge-traces away over on the Mackenzie, he had often thought of this freedom longingly, the wolf blood in him urging him to take it. But he had never quite dared. It thrilled him now. There were no clubs here, no whips, none of the man-beasts whom he had first learned to distrust, and then to hate. It was his misfortune—that quarter-strain of wolf; and the clubs, instead of subduing him, had added to the savagery that was born in him. Men had been his worst enemies. They had beaten him time and again until he was almost dead. They called him "bad," and stepped wide of him, and never missed the chance to snap a whip over his back. His body was covered with scars they had given him.

He had never felt kindness, or love, until the first night the woman had put her warm little hand on his head, and had snuggled her face close down to his, while Thorpe—her husband—had cried out in horror. He had almost buried his fangs in her white flesh, but in an instant her gentle touch, and her sweet voice, had sent through him that wonderful thrill that was his first knowledge of love. And now it was a man who was driving him from her, away from the hand that had never held a club or a whip, and he growled as he trotted deeper into the forest.

He came to the edge of a swamp as day broke. For a time he had been filled with a strange uneasiness, and light did not quite dispel it. At last he was free of men. He could detect nothing that reminded him of their hated presence in the air. But neither could he smell the presence of other dogs, of the sledge, the fire, of companionship and food, and so far back as he could remember they had always been a part of his life.

Here it was very quiet. The swamp lay in a hollow between two ridge-mountains, and the spruce and cedar grew low and thick—so thick that there was almost no snow under them, and day was like twilight. Two things he began to miss more than all others—food and company. Both the wolf and the dog that was in him demanded the first, and that part of him that was dog longed for the latter. To both desires the wolf blood that was strong in him rose responsively. It told him that somewhere in this silent world between the two ridges there was companionship, and that all he had to do to find it was to sit back on his haunches, and cry out his loneliness. More than once something trembled in his deep chest, rose in his throat, and ended there in a whine. It was the wolf howl, not yet quite born.

Food came more easily than voice. Toward midday he cornered a big white rabbit under a log, and killed it. The warm flesh and blood was better than frozen fish, or tallow and bran, and the feast he had gave him confidence. That afternoon he chased many rabbits, and killed two more. Until now, he had never known the delight of pursuing and killing at will, even though he did not eat all he killed.

But there was no fight in the rabbits. They died too easily. They were very sweet and tender to eat, when he was hungry, but the first thrill of killing them passed away after a time. He wanted something bigger. He no longer slunk along as if he were afraid, or as if he wanted to remain hidden. He held his head up. His back bristled. His tail swung free and bushy, like a wolf's. Every hair in his body quivered with the electric energy of life and action. He traveled north and west. It was the call of early days—the days away up on the Mackenzie. The Mackenzie was a thousand miles away.

He came upon many trails in the snow that day, and sniffed the scents left by the hoofs of moose and caribou, and the fur-padded feet of a lynx. He followed a fox, and the trail led him to a place shut in by tall spruce, where the snow was beaten down and reddened with blood. There was an owl's head, feathers, wings and entrails lying here, and he knew that there were other hunters abroad besides himself.

Toward evening he came upon tracks in the snow that were very much like his own. They were quite fresh, and there was a warm scent about them that made him whine, and filled him again with that desire to fall back upon his haunches and send forth the wolf-cry. This desire grew stronger in him as the shadows of night deepened in the forest. He had traveled all day, but he was not tired. There was something about night, now that there were no men near, that exhilarated him strangely. The wolf blood in him ran swifter and swifter. To-night it was clear. The sky was filled with stars. The moon rose. And at last he settled back in the snow and turned his head straight up to the spruce-tops, and the wolf came out of him in a long mournful cry which quivered through the still night for miles.

For a long time he sat and listened after that howl. He had found voice—a voice with a strange new note in it, and it gave him still greater confidence. He had expected an answer, but none came. He had traveled in the face of the wind, and as he howled, a bull moose crashed through the scrub timber ahead of him, his horns rattling against the trees like the tattoo of a clear birch club as he put distance between himself and that cry.

Twice Kazan howled before he went on, and he found joy in the practise of that new note. He came then to the foot of a rough ridge, and turned up out of the swamp to the top of it. The stars and the moon were nearer to him there, and on the other side of the ridge he looked down upon a great sweeping plain, with a frozen lake glistening in the moonlight, and a white river leading from it off into timber that was neither so thick nor so black as that in the swamp.

And then every muscle in his body grew tense, and his blood leaped. From far off in the plain there came a cry. It was *his* cry—the wolf-cry. His jaws snapped. His white fangs gleamed, and he growled deep in his throat. He wanted to reply, but some strange instinct urged him not to. That instinct of the wild was already becoming master of him. In the air, in the whispering of the spruce-tops, in the moon and the stars themselves, there breathed a spirit which told him that what he had heard was the wolf-cry, but that it was not the wolf *call*.

The other came an hour later, clear and distinct, that same wailing howl at the beginning—but ending in a staccato of quick sharp yelps that stirred his blood at once into a fiery excitement that it had never known before. The same instinct told him that this was the call—the hunt-cry. It urged him to come quickly. A few moments later it came again, and this time there was a reply from close down along the foot of the ridge, and another from so far away that Kazan could scarcely hear it. The hunt-pack was gathering for the night chase; but Kazan sat quiet and trembling.

He was not afraid, but he was not ready to go. The ridge seemed to split the world for him. Down there it was new, and strange, and without men. From the other side something seemed pulling him back, and suddenly he turned his head and gazed back through the moonlit space behind him, and whined. It was the dog-whine now. The woman was back there. He could hear her voice. He could feel the touch of her soft hand. He could see the laughter in her face and eyes, the laughter that had made him warm and happy. She was calling to him through the forests, and he was torn between desire to answer that call, and desire to go down into the plain. For he could also see many men waiting for him with clubs, and he could hear the cracking of whips, and feel the sting of their lashes.

For a long time he remained on the top of the ridge that divided his world. And then, at last, he turned and went down into the plain.

All that night he kept close to the hunt-pack, but never quite approached it. This was fortunate for him. He still bore the scent of traces, and of man. The pack would have torn him into pieces. The first instinct of the wild is that of self-preservation. It may have been this, a whisper back through the years of savage forebears, that made Kazan roll in the snow now and then where the feet of the pack had trod the thickest.

That night the pack killed a caribou on the edge of the lake, and feasted until nearly dawn. Kazan hung in the face of the wind. The smell of blood and of warm flesh tickled his nostrils, and his sharp ears could catch the cracking of bones. But the instinct was stronger than the temptation.

Not until broad day, when the pack had scattered far and wide over the plain, did he go boldly to the scene of the kill. He found nothing but an area of blood-reddened snow, covered with bones, entrails and torn bits of tough hide. But it was enough, and he rolled in it, and buried his nose in what was left, and remained all that day close to it, saturating himself with the scent of it.

That night, when the moon and the stars came out again, he sat back with fear and hesitation no longer in him, and announced himself to his new comrades of the great plain.

The pack hunted again that night, or else it was a new pack that started miles to the south, and came up with a doe caribou to the big frozen lake. The night was almost as clear as day, and from the edge of the forest Kazan first saw the caribou run out on the lake a third of a mile away. The pack was about a dozen strong, and had already split into the fatal horseshoe formation, the two leaders running almost abreast of the kill, and slowly closing in.

With a sharp yelp Kazan darted out into the moonlight. He was directly in the path of the fleeing doe, and bore down upon her with lightning speed. Two hundred yards away the doe saw him, and swerved to the right, and the leader on that side met her with open jaws. Kazan was in with the second leader, and leaped at the doe's soft throat. In a snarling mass the pack closed in from behind, and the doe went down, with Kazan half under her body, his fangs sunk deep in her jugular. She lay heavily on him, but he did not lose his hold. It was his first big kill. His blood ran like fire. He snarled between his clamped teeth.

Not until the last quiver had left the body over him did he pull himself out from under her chest and forelegs. He had killed a rabbit that day and was not hungry. So he sat back in the snow and waited, while the ravenous pack tore at the dead doe. After a little he came nearer, nosed in between two of them, and was nipped for his intrusion.

As Kazan drew back, still hesitating to mix with his wild brothers, a big gray form leaped out of the pack and drove straight for his throat. He had just time to throw his shoulder to the attack, and for a moment the two rolled over and over in the snow. They were up before the excitement of sudden battle had drawn the pack from the feast. Slowly they circled about each other, their white fangs bare, their yellowish backs bristling like brushes. The fatal ring of wolves drew about the fighters.

It was not new to Kazan. A dozen times he had sat in rings like this, waiting for the final moment. More than once he had fought for his life within the circle. It was the sledge-dog way of fighting. Unless man interrupted with a club or a whip it always ended in death. Only one fighter could come out alive. Sometimes both died. And there was no man here—only that fatal cordon of waiting white-fanged demons, ready to leap upon and tear to pieces the first of the fighters who was thrown upon his side or back. Kazan was a stranger, but he did not fear those that hemmed him in. The one great law of the pack would compel them to be fair.

He kept his eyes only on the big gray leader who had challenged him. Shoulder to shoulder they continued to circle. Where a few moments before there had been the snapping of jaws and the rending of flesh there was now silence. Soft-footed and soft-throated mongrel dogs from the South would have snarled and growled, but Kazan and the wolf were still, their ears laid forward instead of back, their tails free and bushy.

Suddenly the wolf struck in with the swiftness of lightning, and his jaws came together with the sharpness of steel striking steel. They missed by an inch. In that same instant Kazan darted in to the side, and like knives his teeth gashed the wolf's flank.

They circled again, their eyes growing redder, their lips drawn back until they seemed to have disappeared. And then Kazan leaped for that death-grip at the throat—and missed. It was only by an inch again, and the wolf came back, as he had done, and laid open Kazan's flank so that the blood ran down his leg and reddened the snow. The burn of that flank-wound told Kazan that his enemy was old in the game of fighting. He crouched low, his head straight out, and his throat close to the snow. It was a trick Kazan had learned in puppyhood—to shield his throat, and wait.

Twice the wolf circled about him, and Kazan pivoted slowly, his eyes half closed. A second time the wolf leaped, and Kazan threw up his terrible jaws, sure of that fatal grip just in front of the forelegs. His teeth snapped on empty air. With the nimbleness of a cat the wolf had gone completely over his back.

The trick had failed, and with a rumble of the dog-snarl in his throat, Kazan reached the wolf in a single bound. They met breast to breast. Their fangs clashed and with the whole weight of his body, Kazan flung himself against the wolf's shoulders, cleared his jaws, and struck again for the throat hold. It was another miss—by a hair's breadth—and before he could recover, the wolf's teeth were buried in the back of his neck.

For the first time in his life Kazan felt the terror and the pain of the death-grip, and with a mighty effort he flung his head a little forward and snapped blindly. His powerful jaws closed on the wolf's foreleg, close to the body. There was a cracking of bone and a crunching of flesh, and the circle of waiting wolves grew tense and alert. One or the other of the fighters was sure to go down before the holds were broken, and they but awaited that fatal fall as a signal to leap in to the death.

Only the thickness of hair and hide on the back of Kazan's neck, and the toughness of his muscles, saved him from that terrible fate of the vanquished. The wolf's teeth sank deep, but not deep enough to reach the vital spot, and suddenly Kazan put every ounce of strength in his limbs to the effort, and flung himself up bodily from under his antagonist. The grip on his neck relaxed, and with another rearing leap he tore himself free.

As swift as a whip-lash he whirled on the broken-legged leader of the pack and with the full rush and weight of his shoulders struck him fairly in the side. More deadly than the throat-grip had Kazan sometimes found the lunge when delivered at the right moment. It was deadly now. The big gray wolf lost his feet, rolled upon his back for an instant, and the pack rushed in, eager to rend the last of life from the leader whose power had ceased to exist.

From out of that gray, snarling, bloody-lipped mass, Kazan drew back, panting and bleeding. He was weak. There was a curious sickness in his head. He wanted to lie down in the snow. But the old and infallible instinct warned him not to betray that weakness. From out of the pack a slim, lithe, gray she-wolf came up to him, and lay down in the snow before him, and then rose swiftly and sniffed at his wounds.

She was young and strong and beautiful, but Kazan did not look at her. Where the fight had been he was looking, at what little remained of the old leader. The pack had returned to the feast. He heard again the cracking of bones and the rending of flesh, and something told him that hereafter all the wilderness would hear and recognize his voice, and that when he sat back on his haunches and called to the moon and the stars, those swift-footed hunters of the big plain would respond to it. He circled twice about the caribou and the pack, and then trotted off to the edge of the black spruce forest.

When he reached the shadows he looked back. Gray Wolf was following him. She was only a few yards behind. And now she came up to him, a little timidly, and she, too, looked back to the dark blotch of life out on the lake. And as she stood there close beside him, Kazan sniffed at something in the air that was not the scent of blood, nor the perfume of the balsam and spruce. It was a thing that seemed to come to him from the clear stars, the cloudless moon, the strange and

JAMES OLIVER CURWOOD

beautiful quiet of the night itself. And its presence seemed to be a part of Gray Wolf.

He looked at her, and he found Gray Wolf's eyes alert and questioning. She was young—so young that she seemed scarcely to have passed out of puppyhood. Her body was strong and slim and beautifully shaped. In the moonlight the hair under her throat and along her back shone sleek and soft. She whined at the red staring light in Kazan's eyes, and it was not a puppy's whimper. Kazan moved toward her, and stood with his head over her back, facing the pack. He felt her trembling against his chest. He looked at the moon and the stars again, the mystery of Gray Wolf and of the night throbbing in his blood.

Not much of his life had been spent at the posts. Most of it had been on the trail—in the traces—and the spirit of the mating season had only stirred him from afar. But it was very near now. Gray Wolf lifted her head. Her soft muzzle touched the wound on his neck, and in the gentleness of that touch, in the low sound in her throat, Kazan felt and heard again that wonderful something that had come with the caress of the woman's hand and the sound of her voice.

He turned, whining, his back bristling, his head high and defiant of the wilderness which he faced. Gray Wolf trotted close at his side as they entered into the gloom of the forest.

V

The Fight in the Snow

They found shelter that night under thick balsam, and when they lay down on the soft carpet of needles which the snow had not covered, Gray Wolf snuggled her warm body close to Kazan and licked his wounds. The day broke with a velvety fall of snow, so white and thick that they could not see a dozen leaps ahead of them in the open. It was quite warm, and so still that the whole world seemed filled with only the flutter and whisper of the snowflakes. Through this day Kazan and Gray Wolf traveled side by side. Time and again he turned his head back to the ridge over which he had come, and Gray Wolf could not understand the strange note that trembled in his throat.

In the afternoon they returned to what was left of the caribou doe on the lake. In the edge of the forest Gray Wolf hung back. She did not yet know the meaning of poison-baits, deadfalls and traps, but the instinct of numberless generations was in her veins, and it told her there was danger in visiting a second time a thing that had grown cold in death.

Kazan had seen masters work about carcasses that the wolves had left. He had seen them conceal traps cleverly, and roll little capsules of strychnine in the fat of the entrails, and once he had put a foreleg in a trap, and had experienced its sting and pain and deadly grip. But he did not have Gray Wolf's fear. He urged her to accompany him to the white hummocks on the ice, and at last she went with him and sank back restlessly on her haunches, while he dug out the bones and pieces of flesh that the snow had kept from freezing. But she would not eat, and at last Kazan went and sat on his haunches at her side, and with her looked at what he had dug out from under the snow. He sniffed the air. He could not smell danger, but Gray Wolf told him that it might be there.

She told him many other things in the days and nights that followed. The third night Kazan himself gathered the hunt-pack and led in the chase. Three times that month, before the moon left the skies, he led the chase, and each time there was a kill. But as the snows began to grow softer under his feet he found a greater and greater companionship in

Gray Wolf, and they hunted alone, living on the big white rabbits. In all the world he had loved but two things, the girl with the shining hair and the hands that had caressed him—and Gray Wolf.

He did not leave the big plain, and often He took his mate to the top of the ridge, and he would try to tell her what he had left back there. With the dark nights the call of the woman became so strong upon him that he was filled with a longing to go back, and take Gray Wolf with him.

Something happened very soon after that. They were crossing the open plain one day when up on the face of the ridge Kazan saw something that made his heart stand still. A man, with a dog-sledge and team, was coming down into their world. The wind had not warned them, and suddenly Kazan saw something glisten in the man's hands. He knew what it was. It was the thing that spat fire and thunder, and killed.

He gave his warning to Gray Wolf, and they were off like the wind, side by side. And then came the *sound*—and Kazan's hatred of men burst forth in a snarl as he leaped. There was a queer humming over their heads. The sound from behind came again, and this time Gray Wolf gave a yelp of pain, and rolled over and over in the snow. She was on her feet again in an instant, and Kazan dropped behind her, and ran there until they reached the shelter of the timber. Gray Wolf lay down, and began licking the wound in her shoulder. Kazan faced the ridge. The man was taking up their trail. He stopped where Gray Wolf had fallen, and examined the snow. Then he came on.

Kazan urged Gray Wolf to her feet, and they made for the thick swamp close to the lake. All that day they kept in the face of the wind, and when Gray Wolf lay down Kazan stole back over their trail, watching and sniffing the air.

For days after that Gray Wolf ran lame, and when once they came upon the remains of an old camp, Kazan's teeth were bared in snarling hatred of the man-scent that had been left behind. Growing in him there was a desire for vengeance—vengeance for his own hurts, and for Gray Wolf's. He tried to nose out the man-trail under the cover of fresh snow, and Gray Wolf circled around him anxiously, and tried to lure him deeper into the forest. At last he followed her sullenly. There was a savage redness in his eyes.

Three days later the new moon came. And on the fifth night Kazan struck a trail. It was fresh—so fresh that he stopped as suddenly as though struck by a bullet when he ran upon it, and stood with every muscle in his body quivering, and his hair on end. It was a man-trail. There were the marks of the sledge, the dogs' feet, and the snow-shoeprints of his enemy.

Then he threw up his head to the stars, and from his throat there rolled out over the wide plains the hunt-cry—the wild and savage call for the pack. Never had he put the savagery in it that was there to-night. Again and again he sent forth that call, and then there came an answer and another and still another, until Gray Wolf herself sat back on her haunches and added her voice to Kazan's, and far out on the plain a white and haggard-faced man halted his exhausted dogs to listen, while a voice said faintly from the sledge:

"The wolves, father. Are they coming—after us?"

The man was silent. He was not young. The moon shone in his long white beard, and added grotesquely to the height of his tall gaunt figure. A girl had raised her head from a bearskin pillow on the sleigh. Her dark eyes were filled beautifully with the starlight. She was pale. Her hair fell in a thick shining braid over her shoulder, and she was hugging something tightly to her breast.

"They're on the trail of something—probably a deer," said the man, looking at the breech of his rifle. "Don't worry, Jo. We'll stop at the next bit of scrub and see if we can't find enough dry stuff for a fire.—Wee-ah-h-h-h, boys! Koosh—koosh—" and he snapped his whip over the backs of his team.

From the bundle at the girl's breast there came a small wailing cry. And far back in the plain there answered it the scattered voice of the pack.

At last Kazan was on the trail of vengeance. He ran slowly at first, with Gray Wolf close beside him, pausing every three or four hundred yards to send forth the cry. A gray leaping form joined them from behind. Another followed. Two came in from the side, and Kazan's solitary howl gave place to the wild tongue of the pack. Numbers grew, and with increasing number the pace became swifter. Four—six—seven—ten—fourteen, by the time the more open and wind-swept part of the plain was reached.

It was a strong pack, filled with old and fearless hunters. Gray Wolf was the youngest, and she kept close to Kazan's shoulders. She could see nothing of his red-shot eyes and dripping jaws, and would not have understood if she had seen. But she could *feel* and she was thrilled by the spirit of that strange and mysterious savagery that had made Kazan forget all things but hurt and death.

The pack made no sound. There was only the panting of breath and the soft fall of many feet. They ran swiftly and close. And always Kazan was a leap ahead, with Gray Wolf nosing his shoulder.

Never had he wanted to kill as he felt the desire in him to kill now. For the first time he had no fear of man, no fear of the club, of the whip, or of the thing that blazed forth fire and death. He ran more swiftly, in order to overtake them and give them battle sooner. All of the pent-up madness of four years of slavery and abuse at the hands of men broke loose in thin red streams of fire in his veins, and when at last he saw a moving blotch far out on the plain ahead of him, the cry that came out of his throat was one that Gray Wolf did not understand.

Three hundred yards beyond that moving blotch was the thin line of timber, and Kazan and his followers bore down swiftly. Half-way to the timber they were almost upon it, and suddenly it stopped and became a black and motionless shadow on the snow. From out of it there leaped that lightning tongue of flame that Kazan had always dreaded, and he heard the hissing song of the death-bee over his head. He did not mind it now. He yelped sharply, and the wolves raced in until four of them were neck-and-neck with him.

A second flash—and the death-bee drove from breast to tail of a huge gray fighter close to Gray Wolf. A third—a fourth—a fifth spurt of that fire from the black shadow, and Kazan himself felt a sudden swift passing of a red-hot thing along his shoulder, where the man's last bullet shaved off the hair and stung his flesh.

Three of the pack had gone down under the fire of the rifle, and half of the others were swinging to the right and the left. But Kazan drove straight ahead. Faithfully Gray Wolf followed him.

The sledge-dogs had been freed from their traces, and before he could reach the man, whom he saw with his rifle held like a club in his hands, Kazan was met by the fighting mass of them. He fought like a fiend, and there was the strength and the fierceness of two mates in the mad gnashing of Gray Wolf's fangs. Two of the wolves rushed in, and Kazan heard the terrific, back-breaking thud of the rifle. To him it was the *club*. He wanted to reach it. He wanted to reach the man who held it, and he freed himself from the fighting mass of the dogs and sprang to the sledge. For the first time he saw that there was something human on the sledge, and in an instant he was upon it. He buried his jaws deep. They sank in something soft and hairy, and he opened them for another lunge. And then he heard the voice! It was *her voice*! Every muscle in his body stood still. He became suddenly like flesh turned to lifeless stone.

Her voice! The bear rug was thrown back and what had been hidden under it he saw clearly now in the light of the moon and the stars. In him instinct worked more swiftly than human brain could have given birth to reason. It was not *she*. But the voice was the same, and the white girlish face so close to his own blood-reddened eyes held in it that same mystery that he had learned to love. And he saw now that which she was clutching to her breast, and there came from it a strange thrilling cry—and he knew that here on the sledge he had found not enmity and death, but that from which he had been driven away in the other world beyond the ridge.

In a flash he turned. He snapped at Gray Wolf's flank, and she dropped away with a startled yelp. It had all happened in a moment, but the man was almost down. Kazan leaped under his clubbed rifle and drove into the face of what was left of the pack. His fangs cut like knives. If he had fought like a demon against the dogs, he fought like ten demons now, and the man—bleeding and ready to fall—staggered back to the sledge, marveling at what was happening. For in Gray Wolf there was now the instinct of matehood, and seeing Kazan tearing and righting the pack she joined him in the struggle which she could not understand.

When it was over, Kazan and Gray Wolf were alone out on the plain. The pack had slunk away into the night, and the same moon and stars that had given to Kazan the first knowledge of his birthright told him now that no longer would those wild brothers of the plains respond to his call when he howled into the sky.

He was hurt. And Gray Wolf was hurt, but not so badly as Kazan. He was torn and bleeding. One of his legs was terribly bitten. After a time he saw a fire in the edge of the forest. The old call was strong upon him. He wanted to crawl in to it, and feel the girl's hand on his head, as he had felt that other hand in the world beyond the ridge. He would have gone—and would have urged Gray Wolf to go with him—but the man was there. He whined, and Gray Wolf thrust her warm muzzle against his neck. Something told them both that they were outcasts, that the plains, and the moon, and the stars were against them now, and they slunk into the shelter and the gloom of the forest.

JAMES OLIVER CURWOOD

Kazan could not go far. He could still smell the camp when he lay down. Gray Wolf snuggled close to him. Gently she soothed with her soft tongue Kazan's bleeding wounds. And Kazan, lifting his head, whined softly to the stars.

VI

Joan

On the edge of the cedar and spruce forest old Pierre Radisson built the fire. He was bleeding from a dozen wounds, where the fangs of the wolves had reached to his flesh, and he felt in his breast that old and terrible pain, of which no one knew the meaning but himself. He dragged in log after log, piled them on the fire until the flames leaped tip to the crisping needles of the limbs above, and heaped a supply close at hand for use later in the night.

From the sledge Joan watched him, still wild-eyed and fearful, still trembling. She was holding her baby close to her breast. Her long heavy hair smothered her shoulders and arms in a dark lustrous veil that glistened and rippled in the firelight when she moved. Her young face was scarcely a woman's to-night, though she was a mother. She looked like a child.

Old Pierre laughed as he threw down the last armful of fuel, and stood breathing hard.

"It was close, *ma cheri*," he panted through his white beard. "We were nearer to death out there on the plain than we will ever be again, I hope. But we are comfortable now, and warm. Eh? You are no longer afraid?"

He sat down beside his daughter, and gently pulled back the soft fur that enveloped the bundle she held in her arms. He could see one pink cheek of baby Joan. The eyes of Joan, the mother, were like stars.

"It was the baby who saved us," she whispered. "The dogs were being torn to pieces by the wolves, and I saw them leaping upon you, when one of them sprang to the sledge. At first I thought it was one of the dogs. But it was a wolf. He tore once at us, and the bearskin saved us. He was almost at my throat when baby cried, and then he stood there, his red eyes a foot from us, and I could have sworn again that he was a dog. In an instant he turned, and was fighting the wolves. I saw him leap upon one that was almost at your throat."

"He *was* a dog," said old Pierre, holding out his hands to the warmth. "They often wander away from the posts, and join the wolves. I have had dogs do that. *Ma cheri*, a dog is a dog all his life. Kicks, abuse, even the wolves can not change him—for long. He was one of the pack. He came with them—to kill. But when he found *us*—"

"He fought for us," breathed the girl. She gave him the bundle, and stood up, straight and tall and slim in the firelight. "He fought for us— and he was terribly hurt," she said. "I saw him drag himself away. Father, if he is out there—dying—"

Pierre Radisson stood up. He coughed in a shuddering way, trying to stifle the sound under his beard. The fleck of crimson that came to his lips with the cough Joan did not see. She had seen nothing of it during the six days they had been traveling up from the edge of civilization. Because of that cough, and the stain that came with it, Pierre had made more than ordinary haste.

"I have been thinking of that," he said. "He was badly hurt, and I do not think he went far. Here—take little Joan and sit close to the fire until I come back."

The moon and the stars were brilliant in the sky when he went out in the plain. A short distance from the edge of the timber-line he stood for a moment upon the spot where the wolves had overtaken them an hour before. Not one of his four dogs had lived. The snow was red with their blood, and their bodies lay stiff where they had fallen under the pack. Pierre shuddered as he looked at them. If the wolves had not turned their first mad attack upon the dogs, what would have become of himself, Joan and the baby? He turned away, with another of those hollow coughs that brought the blood to his lips.

A few yards to one side he found in the snow the trail of the strange dog that had come with the wolves, and had turned against them in that moment when all seemed lost. It was not a clean running trail. It was more of a furrow in the snow, and Pierre Radisson followed it, expecting to find the dog dead at the end of it.

In the sheltered spot to which he had dragged himself in the edge of the forest Kazan lay for a long time after the fight, alert and watchful. He felt no very great pain. But he had lost the power to stand upon his legs. His flanks seemed paralyzed. Gray Wolf crouched close at his side, sniffing the air. They could smell the camp, and Kazan could detect the two things that were there—*man* and *woman*. He knew that the girl was there, where he could see the glow of the firelight through the spruce and the cedars. He wanted to go to her. He wanted to drag himself close in to the fire, and take Gray Wolf with him, and listen to her voice, and feel the touch of her hand. But the man was there, and to him man had always meant the club, the whip, pain, death.

Gray Wolf crouched close to his side, and whined softly as she urged Kazan to flee deeper with her into the forest. At last she understood that he could not move, and she ran nervously out into the plain, and back again, until her footprints were thick in the trail she made. The instincts of matehood were strong in her. It was she who first saw Pierre Radisson coming over their trail, and she ran swiftly back to Kazan and gave the warning.

Then Kazan caught the scent, and he saw the shadowy figure coming through the starlight. He tried to drag himself back, but he could move only by inches. The man came rapidly nearer. Kazan caught the glisten of the rifle in his hand. He heard his hollow cough, and the tread of his feet in the snow. Gray Wolf crouched shoulder to shoulder with him, trembling and showing her teeth. When Pierre had approached within fifty feet of them she slunk back into the deeper shadows of the spruce.

Kazan's fangs were bared menacingly when Pierre stopped and looked down at him. With an effort he dragged himself to his feet, but fell back into the snow again. The man leaned his rifle against a sapling and bent over him fearlessly. With a fierce growl Kazan snapped at his extended hands. To his surprise the man did not pick up a stick or a club. He held out his hand again—cautiously—and spoke in a voice new to Kazan. The dog snapped again, and growled.

The man persisted, talking to him all the time, and once his mittened hand touched Kazan's head, and escaped before the jaws could reach it. Again and again the man reached out his hand, and three times Kazan felt the touch of it, and there was neither threat nor hurt in it. At last Pierre turned away and went back over the trail.

When he was out of sight and hearing, Kazan whined, and the crest along his spine flattened. He looked wistfully toward the glow of the fire. The man had not hurt him, and the three-quarters of him that was dog wanted to follow.

Gray Wolf came back, and stood with stiffly planted forefeet at his side. She had never been this near to man before, except when the pack had overtaken the sledge out on the plain. She could not understand. Every instinct that was in her warned her that he was the most dangerous of all things, more to be feared than the strongest beasts, the storms, the floods, cold and starvation. And yet this man had not harmed her mate. She sniffed at Kazan's back and head, where the mittened hand had touched. Then she trotted back into the darkness again, for beyond the edge of the forest she once more saw moving life.

The man was returning, and with him was the girl. Her voice was soft and sweet, and there was about her the breath and sweetness of woman. The man stood prepared, but not threatening.

"Be careful, Joan," he warned.

She dropped on her knees in the snow, just out of reach.

"Come, boy—come!" she said gently. She held out her hand. Kazan's muscles twitched. He moved an inch—two inches toward her. There was the old light in her eyes and face now, the love and gentleness he had known once before, when another woman with shining hair and eyes had come into his life. "Come!" she whispered as she saw him move, and she bent a little, reached a little farther with her hand, and at last touched his head.

Pierre knelt beside her. He was proffering something, and Kazan smelled meat. But it was the girl's hand that made him tremble and shiver, and when she drew back, urging him to follow her, he dragged himself painfully a foot or two through the snow. Not until then did the girl see his mangled leg. In an instant she had forgotten all caution, and was down close at his side.

"He can't walk," she cried, a sudden tremble in her voice. "Look, *mon père!* Here is a terrible cut. We must carry him."

"I guessed that much," replied Radisson. "For that reason I brought the blanket. *Mon Dieu*, listen to that!"

From the darkness of the forest there came a low wailing cry.

Kazan lifted his head and a trembling whine answered in his throat. It was Gray Wolf calling to him.

It was a miracle that Pierre Radisson should put the blanket about Kazan, and carry him in to the camp, without scratch or bite. It was this miracle that he achieved, with Joan's arm resting on Kazan's shaggy neck as she held one end of the blanket. They laid him down close to the fire, and after a little it was the man again who brought warm water and washed away the blood from the torn leg, and then put something on it that was soft and warm and soothing, and finally bound a cloth about it.

All this was strange and new to Kazan. Pierre's hand, as well as the girl's, stroked his head. It was the man who brought him a gruel of meal and tallow, and urged him to eat, while Joan sat with her chin in her two hands, looking at the dog, and talking to him. After this, when he was quite comfortable, and no longer afraid, he heard a strange small cry from the furry bundle on the sledge that brought his head up with a jerk.

Joan saw the movement, and heard the low answering whimper in his throat. She turned quickly to the bundle, talking and cooing to it as she took it in her arms, and then she pulled back the bearskin so that Kazan could see. He had never seen a baby before, and Joan held it out before him, so that he could look straight at it and see what a wonderful creature it was. Its little pink face stared steadily at Kazan. Its tiny fists reached out, and it made queer little sounds at him, and then suddenly it kicked and screamed with delight and laughed. At those sounds Kazan's whole body relaxed, and he dragged himself to the girl's feet.

"See, he likes the baby!" she cried. "*Mon père*, we must give him a name. What shall it be?"

"Wait till morning for that," replied the father. "It is late, Joan. Go into the tent, and sleep. We have no dogs now, and will travel slowly. So we must start early."

With her hand on the tent-flap, Joan, turned.

"He came with the wolves," she said. "Let us call him Wolf." With one arm she was holding the little Joan. The other she stretched out to Kazan. "Wolf! Wolf!" she called softly.

Kazan's eyes were on her. He knew that she was speaking to him, and he drew himself a foot toward her.

"He knows it already!" she cried. "Good night, *mon père*."

For a long time after she had gone into the tent, old Pierre Radisson sat on the edge of the sledge, facing the fire, with Kazan at his feet. Suddenly the silence was broken again by Gray Wolf's lonely howl deep in the forest. Kazan lifted his head and whined.

"She's calling for you, boy," said Pierre understandingly.

He coughed, and clutched a hand to his breast, where the pain seemed rending him.

"Frost-bitten lung," he said, speaking straight at Kazan. "Got it early in the winter, up at Fond du Lac. Hope we'll get home—in time—with the kids."

In the loneliness and emptiness of the big northern wilderness one falls into the habit of talking to one's self. But Kazan's head was alert, and his eyes watchful, so Pierre spoke to him.

"We've got to get them home, and there's only you and me to do it," he said, twisting his beard. Suddenly he clenched his fists.

His hollow racking cough convulsed him again.

"Home!" he panted, clutching his chest. "It's eighty miles straight

JAMES OLIVER CURWOOD

north—to the Churchill—and I pray to God we'll get there—with the kids—before my lungs give out."

He rose to his feet, and staggered a little as he walked. There was a collar about Kazan's neck, and he chained him to the sledge. After that he dragged three or four small logs upon the fire, and went quietly into the tent where Joan and the baby were already asleep. Several times that night Kazan heard the distant voice of Gray Wolf calling for him, but something told him that he must not answer it now. Toward dawn Gray Wolf came close in to the camp, and for the first time Kazan replied to her.

His howl awakened the man. He came out of the tent, peered for a few moments up at the sky, built up the fire, and began to prepare breakfast. He patted Kazan on the head, and gave him a chunk of meat. Joan came out a few moments later, leaving the baby asleep in the tent. She ran up and kissed Pierre, and then dropped down on her knees beside Kazan, and talked to him almost as he had heard her talk to the baby. When she jumped up to help her father, Kazan followed her, and when Joan saw him standing firmly upon his legs she gave a cry of pleasure.

It was a strange journey that began into the North that day. Pierre Radisson emptied the sledge of everything but the tent, blankets, food and the furry nest for baby Joan. Then he harnessed himself in the traces and dragged the sledge over the snow. He coughed incessantly.

"It's a cough I've had half the winter," lied Pierre, careful that Joan saw no sign of blood on his lips or beard. "I'll keep in the cabin for a week when we get home."

Even Kazan, with that strange beast knowledge which man, unable to explain, calls instinct, knew that what he said was not the truth. Perhaps it was largely because he had heard other men cough like this, and that for generations his sledge-dog ancestors had heard men cough as Radisson coughed—and had learned what followed it.

More than once he had scented death in tepees and cabins, which he had not entered, and more than once he had sniffed at the mystery of death that was not quite present, but near—just as he had caught at a distance the subtle warning of storm and of fire. And that strange thing seemed to be very near to him now, as he followed at the end of his chain behind the sledge. It made him restless, and half a dozen times, when the sledge stopped, he sniffed at the bit of humanity buried in the bearskin. Each time that he did this Joan was quickly at his side, and twice she patted his scarred and grizzled head until every drop of blood in his body leaped riotously with a joy which his body did not reveal.

This day the chief thing that he came to understand was that the little creature on the sledge was very precious to the girl who stroked his head and talked to him, and that it was very helpless. He learned, too, that Joan was most delighted, and that her voice was softer and thrilled him more deeply, when he paid attention to that little, warm, living thing in the bearskin.

For a long time after they made camp Pierre Radisson sat beside the fire. To-night he did not smoke. He stared straight into the flames. When at last he rose to go into the tent with the girl and the baby, he bent over Kazan and examined his hurt.

"You've got to work in the traces to-morrow, boy," he said. "We must make the river by to-morrow night. If we don't—"

He did not finish. He was choking back one of those tearing coughs when the tent-flap dropped behind him. Kazan lay stiff and alert, his eyes filled with a strange anxiety. He did not like to see Radisson enter the tent, for stronger than ever there hung that oppressive mystery in the air about him, and it seemed to be a part of Pierre.

Three times that night he heard faithful Gray Wolf calling for him deep in the forest, and each time he answered her. Toward dawn she came in close to camp. Once he caught the scent of her when she circled around in the wind, and he tugged and whined at the end of his chain, hoping that she would come in and lie down at his side. But no sooner had Radisson moved in the tent than Gray Wolf was gone. The man's face was thinner, and his eyes were redder this morning. His cough was not so loud or so rending. It was like a wheeze, as if something had given way inside, and before the girl came out he clutched his hands often at his throat. Joan's face whitened when she saw him. Anxiety gave way to fear in her eyes. Pierre Radisson laughed when she flung her arms about him, and coughed to prove that what he said was true.

"You see the cough is not so bad, my Joan," he said. "It is breaking up. You can not have forgotten, *ma cheri*? It always leaves one red-eyed and weak."

It was a cold bleak dark day that followed, and through it Kazan and the man tugged at the fore of the sledge, with Joan following in the trail behind. Kazan's wound no longer hurt him. He pulled steadily with all his splendid strength, and the man never lashed him once, but patted him with his mittened hand on head and back. The day grew steadily darker and in the tops of the trees there was the low moaning of a storm.

Darkness and the coming of the storm did not drive Pierre Radisson into camp. "We must reach the river," he said to himself over and over again. "We must reach the river—we must reach the river—" And he steadily urged Kazan on to greater effort, while his own strength at the end of the traces grew less.

It had begun to storm when Pierre stopped to build a fire at noon. The snow fell straight down in a white deluge so thick that it hid the tree trunks fifty yards away. Pierre laughed when Joan shivered and snuggled close up to him with the baby in her arms. He waited only an hour, and then fastened Kazan in the traces again, and buckled the straps once more about his own waist. In the silent gloom that was almost night Pierre carried his compass in his hand, and at last, late in the afternoon, they came to a break in the timber-line, and ahead of them lay a plain, across which Radisson pointed an exultant hand.

"There's the river, Joan," he said, his voice faint and husky. "We can camp here now and wait for the storm to pass."

Under a thick clump of spruce he put up the tent, and then began gathering fire-wood. Joan helped him. As soon as they had boiled coffee and eaten a supper of meat and toasted biscuits, Joan went into the tent and dropped exhausted on her thick bed of balsam boughs, wrapping herself and the baby up close in the skins and blankets. To-night she had no word for Kazan. And Pierre was glad that she was too tired to sit beside the fire and talk. And yet—

Kazan's alert eyes saw Pierre start suddenly. He rose from his seat on the sledge and went to the tent. He drew back the flap and thrust in his head and shoulders.

"Asleep, Joan?" he asked.

"Almost, father. Won't you please come—soon?"

"After I smoke," he said. "Are you comfortable?"

"Yes, I'm so tired—and—sleepy—"

Pierre laughed softly. In the darkness he was gripping at his throat.

"We're almost home, Joan. That is our river out there—the Little Beaver. If I should run away and leave you to-night you could follow it right to our cabin. It's only forty miles. Do you hear?"

"Yes—I know—"

"Forty miles—straight down the river. You couldn't lose yourself, Joan. Only you'd have to be careful of air-holes in the ice."

"Won't you come to bed, father? You're tired—and almost sick."

"Yes—after I smoke," he repeated. "Joan, will you keep reminding me to-morrow of the air-holes? I might forget. You can always tell them, for the snow and the crust over them are whiter than that on the rest of the ice, and like a sponge. Will you remember—the airholes—"

"Yes-s-s-s—"

Pierre dropped the tent-flap and returned to the fire. He staggered as he walked.

"Good night, boy," he said. "Guess I'd better go in with the kids. Two days more—forty miles—two days—"

Kazan watched him as he entered the tent. He laid his weight against the end of his chain until the collar shut off his wind. His legs and back twitched. In that tent where Radisson had gone were Joan and the baby. He knew that Pierre would not hurt them, but he knew also that with Pierre Radisson something terrible and impending was hovering very near to them. He wanted the man outside—by the fire—where he could lie still, and watch him.

In the tent there was silence. Nearer to him than before came Gray Wolf's cry. Each night she was calling earlier, and coming closer to the camp. He wanted her very near to him to-night, but he did not even whine in response. He dared not break that strange silence in the tent. He lay still for a long time, tired and lame from the day's journey, but sleepless. The fire burned lower; the wind in the tree-tops died away; and the thick gray clouds rolled like a massive curtain from under the skies. The stars began to glow white and metallic, and from far in the North there came faintly a crisping moaning sound, like steel sleigh-runners running over frosty snow—the mysterious monotone of the Northern Lights. After that it grew steadily and swiftly colder.

To-night Gray Wolf did not compass herself by the direction of the wind. She followed like a sneaking shadow over the trail Pierre Radisson had made, and when Kazan heard her again, long after midnight, he lay with, his head erect, and his body rigid, save for a curious twitching of his muscles. There was a new note in Gray Wolf's voice, a wailing note in which there was more than the mate-call. It was The Message. And at the sound of it Kazan rose from out of his silence and his fear, and with his head turned straight up to the sky he howled as the wild dogs of the North howl before the tepees of masters who are newly dead.

Pierre Radisson was dead.

VII

OUT OF THE BLIZZARD

It was dawn when the baby snuggled close to Joan's warm breast and awakened her with its cry of hunger. She opened her eyes, brushed back the thick hair from her face, and could see where the shadowy form of her father was lying at the other side of the tent. He was very quiet, and she was pleased that he was still sleeping. She knew that the day before he had been very near to exhaustion, and so for half an hour longer she lay quiet, cooing softly to the baby Joan. Then she arose cautiously, tucked the baby in the warm blankets and furs, put on her heavier garments, and went outside.

By this time it was broad day, and she breathed a sigh of relief when she saw that the storm had passed. It was bitterly cold. It seemed to her that she had never known it to be so cold in all her life. The fire was completely out. Kazan was huddled in a round ball, his nose tucked under his body. He raised his head, shivering, as Joan came out. With her heavily moccasined foot Joan scattered the ashes and charred sticks where the fire had been. There was not a spark left. In returning to the tent she stopped for a moment beside Kazan, and patted his shaggy head.

"Poor Wolf!" she said. "I wish I had given you one of the bearskins!"

She threw back the tent-flap and entered. For the first time she saw her father's face in the light—and outside, Kazan heard the terrible moaning cry that broke from her lips. No one could have looked at Pierre Radisson's face once—and not have understood.

After that one agonizing cry, Joan flung herself upon her father's breast, sobbing so softly that even Kazan's sharp ears heard no sound. She remained there in her grief until every vital energy of womanhood and motherhood in her girlish body was roused to action by the wailing cry of baby Joan. Then she sprang to her feet and ran out through the tent opening. Kazan tugged at the end of his chain to meet her, but she saw nothing of him now. The terror of the wilderness is greater than that of death, and in an instant it had fallen upon Joan. It was not because of fear for herself. It was the baby. The wailing cries from the tent pierced her like knife-thrusts.

And then, all at once, there came to her what old Pierre had said the night before—his words about the river, the air-holes, the home forty miles away. *"You couldn't lose yourself, Joan"* He had guessed what might happen.

She bundled the baby deep in the furs and returned to the fire-bed. Her one thought now was that they must have fire. She made a little pile of birch-bark, covered it with half-burned bits of wood, and went into the tent for the matches. Pierre Radisson carried them in a waterproof box in a pocket of his bearskin coat. She sobbed as she kneeled beside him again, and obtained the box. As the fire flared up she added other bits of wood, and then some of the larger pieces that Pierre had dragged into camp. The fire gave her courage. Forty miles—and the river led to their home! She must make that, with the baby and Wolf. For the first time she turned to him, and spoke his name as she put her hand on his head. After that she gave him a chunk of meat which she thawed out over the fire, and melted the snow for tea. She was not hungry, but she recalled how her father had made her eat four or five times a day, so she forced herself to make a breakfast of a biscuit, a shred of meat and as much hot tea as she could drink.

The terrible hour she dreaded followed that. She wrapped blankets closely about her father's body, and tied them with babiche cord. After that she piled all the furs and blankets that remained on the sledge close to the fire, and snuggled baby Joan deep down in them. Pulling down the tent was a task. The ropes were stiff and frozen, and when she had finished, one of her hands was bleeding. She piled the tent on the sledge, and then, half, covering her face, turned and looked back.

Pierre Radisson lay on his balsam bed, with nothing over him now but the gray sky and the spruce-tops. Kazan stood stiff-legged and sniffed the air. His spine bristled when Joan went back slowly and kneeled beside the blanket-wrapped object. When she returned to him her face was white and tense, and now there was a strange and terrible look in her eyes as she stared out across the barren. She put him in the traces, and fastened about her slender waist the strap that Pierre had used. Thus they struck out for the river, floundering knee-deep in the freshly fallen and drifted snow. Half-way Joan stumbled in a drift and fell, her loose hair flying in a shimmering veil over the snow. With a mighty pull Kazan was at her side, and his cold muzzle touched her face as she drew herself to her feet. For a moment Joan took his shaggy head between her two hands.

"Wolf!" she moaned. "Oh, Wolf!"

She went on, her breath coming pantingly now, even from her brief exertion. The snow was not so deep on the ice of the river. But a wind was rising. It came from the north and east, straight in her face, and Joan bowed her head as she pulled with Kazan. Half a mile down the river she stopped, and no longer could she repress the hopelessness that rose to her lips in a sobbing choking cry. Forty miles! She clutched her hands at her breast, and stood breathing like one who had been beaten, her back to the wind. The baby was quiet. Joan went back and peered down under the furs, and what she saw there spurred her on again almost fiercely. Twice she stumbled to her knees in the drifts during the next quarter of a mile.

After that there was a stretch of wind-swept ice, and Kazan pulled the sledge alone. Joan walked at his side. There was a pain in her chest. A thousand needles seemed pricking her face, and suddenly she remembered the thermometer. She exposed it for a time on the top of the tent. When she looked at it a few minutes later it was thirty degrees below zero. Forty miles! And her father had told her that she could make it—and could not lose herself! But she did not know that even her father would have been afraid to face the north that day, with the temperature at thirty below, and a moaning wind bringing the first warning of a blizzard.

The timber was far behind her now. Ahead there was nothing but the pitiless barren, and the timber beyond that was hidden by the gray gloom of the day. If there had been trees, Joan's heart would not have choked so with terror. But there was nothing—nothing but that gray ghostly gloom, with the rim of the sky touching the earth a mile away.

The snow grew heavy under her feet again. Always she was watching for those treacherous, frost-coated traps in the ice her father had spoken of. But she found now that all the ice and snow looked alike to her, and that there was a growing pain back of her eyes. It was the intense cold.

The river widened into a small lake, and here the wind struck her in the face with such force that her weight was taken from the strap, and Kazan dragged the sledge alone. A few inches of snow impeded her as much as a foot had done before. Little by little she dropped back. Kazan forged to her side, every ounce of his magnificent strength in the traces. By the time they were on the river channel again, Joan was at the back of the sledge, following in the trail made by Kazan. She was powerless to help him. She felt more and more the leaden weight of her legs. There was but one hope—and that was the forest. If they did not reach it soon, within half an hour, she would be able to go no farther. Over and over again she moaned a prayer for her baby as she struggled on. She fell in the snow-drifts. Kazan and the sledge became only a dark blotch to her. And then, all at once, she saw that they were leaving her. They were not more than twenty feet ahead of her—but the blotch seemed to be a vast distance away. Every bit of life and strength in her body was now bent upon reaching the sledge—and baby Joan.

It seemed an interminable time before she gained. With the sledge only six feet ahead of her she struggled for what seemed to her to be an hour before she could reach out and touch it. With a moan she flung herself forward, and fell upon it. She no longer heard the wailing of the storm. She no longer felt discomfort. With her face in the furs under which baby Joan was buried, there came to her with swiftness and joy a vision of warmth and home. And then the vision faded away, and was followed by deep night.

Kazan stopped in the trail. He came back then and sat down upon his haunches beside her, waiting for her to move and speak. But she was very still. He thrust his nose into her loose hair. A whine rose in his throat, and suddenly he raised his head and sniffed in the face of the wind. Something came to him with that wind. He muzzled Joan again, hut she did not stir. Then he went forward, and stood in his traces, ready for the pull, and looked hack at her. Still she did not move or speak, and Kazan's whine gave place to a sharp excited bark.

The strange thing in the wind came to him stronger for a moment. He began to pull. The sledge-runners had frozen to the snow, and it took every ounce of his strength to free them. Twice during the next five minutes he stopped and sniffed the air. The third time that he halted, in a drift of snow, he returned to Joan's side again, and whined to awaken her. Then he tugged again at the end of his traces, and foot by foot he dragged the sledge through the drift. Beyond the drift there was a stretch of clear ice, and here Kazan rested. During a lull in the wind the scent came to him stronger than before.

At the end of the clear ice was a narrow break in the shore, where a creek ran into the main stream. If Joan had been conscious she would have urged him straight ahead. But Kazan turned into the break, and for ten minutes he struggled through the snow without a rest, whining more and more frequently, until at last the whine broke into a joyous bark. Ahead of him, close to the creek, was a small cabin. Smoke was rising out of the chimney. It was the scent of smoke that had come to him in the wind. A hard level slope reached to the cabin door, and with the last strength that was in him Kazan dragged his burden up that. Then he settled himself back beside Joan, lifted his shaggy head to the dark sky and howled.

A moment later the door opened. A man came out. Kazan's reddened, snow-shot eyes followed him watchfully as he ran to the sledge. He heard his startled exclamation as he bent over Joan. In another lull of the wind there came from out of the mass of furs on the sledge the wailing, half-smothered voice of baby Joan.

A deep sigh of relief heaved up from Kazan's chest. He was exhausted. His strength was gone. His feet were torn and bleeding. But the voice of baby Joan filled him with a strange happiness, and he lay down in his traces, while the man carried Joan and the baby into the life and warmth of the cabin.

A few minutes later the man reappeared. He was not old, like Pierre Radisson. He came close to Kazan, and looked down at him.

"My God," he said. "And you did that—*alone!*"

He bent down fearlessly, unfastened him from the traces, and led him toward the cabin door. Kazan hesitated but once—almost on the threshold. He turned his head, swift and alert. From out of the moaning and wailing of the storm it seemed to him that for a moment he had heard the voice of Gray Wolf.

Then the cabin door closed behind him.

Back in a shadowy corner of the cabin he lay, while the man prepared something over a hot stove for Joan. It was a long time before Joan rose from the cot on which the man had placed her. After that Kazan heard her sobbing; and then the man made her eat, and for a time they talked. Then the stranger hung up a big blanket in front of the bunk, and sat down close to the stove. Quietly Kazan slipped along the wall, and crept under the bunk. For a long time he could hear the sobbing breath of the girl. Then all was still.

The next morning he slipped out through the door when the man opened it, and sped swiftly into the forest. Half a mile away he found the trail of Gray Wolf, and called to her. From the frozen river came her reply, and he went to her.

Vainly Gray Wolf tried to lure him back into their old haunts— away from the cabin and the scent of man. Late that morning the man harnessed his dogs, and from the fringe of the forest Kazan saw him tuck Joan and the baby among the furs on the sledge, as old Pierre had done. All that day he followed in the trail of the team, with Gray Wolf slinking behind him. They traveled until dark; and then, under the stars and the moon that had followed the storm, the man still urged on his team. It was deep in the night when they came to another cabin, and the man beat upon the door. A light, the opening of the door, the joyous welcome of a man's voice, Joan's sobbing cry—Kazan heard these from the shadows in which he was hidden, and then slipped back to Gray Wolf.

In the days and weeks that followed Joan's home-coming the lure of the cabin and of the woman's hand held Kazan. As he had tolerated Pierre, so now he tolerated the younger man who lived with Joan and the baby. He knew that the man was very dear to Joan, and that the baby was very dear to him, as it was to the girl. It was not until the third day that Joan succeeded in coaxing him into the cabin—and that was the day on which the man returned with the dead and frozen body of Pierre. It was Joan's husband who first found the name on the collar he wore, and they began calling him Kazan.

Half a mile away, at the summit of a huge mass of rock which the Indians called the Sun Rock, he and Gray Wolf had found a home; and from here they went down to their hunts on the plain, and often the girl's voice reached up to them, calling, "*Kazan! Kazan! Kazan!*"

Through all the long winter Kazan hovered thus between the lure of Joan and the cabin—and Gray Wolf.

Then came Spring—and the Great Change.

VIII

THE GREAT CHANGE

The rocks, the ridges and the valleys were taking on a warmer glow. The poplar buds were ready to burst. The scent of balsam and of spruce grew heavier in the air each day, and all through the wilderness, in plain and forest, there was the rippling murmur of the spring floods finding their way to Hudson's Bay. In that great bay there was the rumble and crash of the ice fields thundering down in the early breakup through the Roes Welcome—the doorway to the Arctic, and for that reason there still came with the April wind an occasional sharp breath of winter.

Kazan had sheltered himself against that wind. Not a breath of air stirred in the sunny spot the wolf-dog had chosen for himself. He was more comfortable than he had been at any time during the six months of terrible winter—and as he slept he dreamed.

Gray Wolf, his wild mate, lay near him, flat on her belly, her forepaws reaching out, her eyes and nostrils as keen and alert as the smell of man could make them. For there was that smell of man, as well as of balsam and spruce, in the warm spring air. She gazed anxiously and sometimes steadily, at Kazan as he slept. Her own gray spine stiffened when she saw the tawny hair along Kazan's back bristle at some dream vision. She whined softly as his upper lip snarled back, showing his long white fangs. But for the most part Kazan lay quiet, save for the muscular twitchings of legs, shoulders and muzzle, which always tell when a dog is dreaming; and as he dreamed there came to the door of the cabin out on the plain a blue-eyed girl-woman, with a big brown braid over her shoulder, who called through the cup of her hands, "Kazan, Kazan, Kazan!"

The voice reached faintly to the top of the Sun Rock, and Gray Wolf flattened her ears. Kazan stirred, and in another instant he was awake and on his feet. He leaped to an outcropping ledge, sniffing the air and looking far out over the plain that lay below them.

Over the plain the woman's voice came to them again, and Kazan ran to the edge of the rock and whined. Gray Wolf stepped softly to his side and laid her muzzle on his shoulder. She had grown to know what the Voice meant. Day and night she feared it, more than she feared the scent or sound of man.

Since she had given up the pack and her old life for Kazan, the Voice had become Gray Wolf's greatest enemy, and she hated it. It took Kazan from her. And wherever it went, Kazan followed.

Night after night it robbed her of her mate, and left her to wander alone under the stars and the moon, keeping faithfully to her loneliness, and never once responding with her own tongue to the hunt-calls of her wild brothers and sisters in the forests and out on the plains. Usually she would snarl at the Voice, and sometimes nip Kazan lightly to show her displeasure. But to-day, as the Voice came a third time, she slunk back into the darkness of a fissure between two rocks, and Kazan saw only the fiery glow of her eyes.

Kazan ran nervously to the trail their feet had worn up to the top of the Sun Rock, and stood undecided. All day, and yesterday, he had been uneasy and disturbed. Whatever it was that stirred him seemed to be in the air, for he could not see it or hear it or scent it. But he could *feel* it. He went to the fissure and sniffed at Gray Wolf. Usually she whined coaxingly. But her response to-day was to draw back her lips until he could see her white fangs.

A fourth tune the Voice came to them faintly, and she snapped fiercely at some unseen thing in the darkness between the two rocks. Kazan went again to the trail, still hesitating. Then he began to go down. It was a narrow winding trail, worn only by the pads and claws of animals, for the Sun Rock was a huge crag that rose almost sheer up for a hundred feet above the tops of the spruce and balsam, its bald crest catching the first gleams of the sun in the morning and the last glow of it in the evening. Gray Wolf had first led Kazan to the security of the retreat at the top of the rock.

When he reached the bottom he no longer hesitated, but darted swiftly in the direction of the cabin. Because of that instinct of the wild that was still in him, he always approached the cabin with caution. He never gave warning, and for a moment Joan was startled when she looked up from her baby and saw Kazan's shaggy head and shoulders in the open door. The baby struggled and kicked in her delight, and held out her two hands with cooing cries to Kazan. Joan, too, held out a hand.

"Kazan!" she cried softly. "Come in, Kazan!"

Slowly the wild red light in Kazan's eyes softened. He put a forefoot on the sill, and stood there, while the girl urged him again. Suddenly his legs seemed to sink a little under him, his tail drooped and he slunk in with that doggish air of having committed a crime. The creatures he loved were in the cabin, but the cabin itself he hated. He hated all cabins, for they all breathed of the club and the whip and bondage. Like all sledge-dogs he preferred the open snow for a bed, and the spruce-tops for shelter.

Joan dropped her hand to his head, and at its touch there thrilled through him that strange joy that was his reward for leaving Gray Wolf and the wild. Slowly he raised his head until his black muzzle rested on her lap, and he closed his eyes while that wonderful little creature that mystified him so—the baby—prodded him with her tiny feet, and pulled his tawny hair. He loved these baby-maulings even more than the touch of Joan's hand.

Motionless, sphinx-like, undemonstrative in every muscle of his body, Kazan stood, scarcely breathing. More than once this lack of demonstration had urged Joan's husband to warn her. But the wolf that was in Kazan, his wild aloofness, even his mating with Gray Wolf had made her love him more. She understood, and had faith in him.

In the days of the last snow Kazan had proved himself. A neighboring trapper had run over with his team, and the baby Joan had toddled up to one of the big huskies. There was a fierce snap of jaws, a scream of horror from Joan, a shout from the men as they leaped toward the pack. But Kazan was ahead of them all. In a gray streak that traveled with the speed of a bullet he was at the big husky's throat. When they pulled him off, the husky was dead. Joan thought of that now, as the baby kicked and tousled Kazan's head.

"Good old Kazan," she cried softly, putting her face down close to him. "We're glad you came, Kazan, for we're going to be alone to-night—baby and I. Daddy's gone to the post, and you must care for us while he's away."

She tickled his nose with the end of her long shining braid. This always delighted the baby, for in spite of his stoicism Kazan had to sniff and sometimes to sneeze, and twig his ears. And it pleased him, too. He loved the sweet scent of Joan's hair.

"And you'd fight for us, if you had to, wouldn't you?" she went on. Then she rose quietly. "I must close the door," she said. "I don't want you to go away again to-day, Kazan. You must stay with us."

Kazan went off to his corner, and lay down. Just as there had been some strange thing at the top of the Sun Rock to disturb him that day, so now there was a mystery that disturbed him in the cabin. He sniffed the air, trying to fathom its secret. Whatever it was, it seemed to make his mistress different, too. And she was digging out all sorts of odds and ends of things about the cabin, and doing them up in packages. Late that night, before she went to bed, Joan came and snuggled her hand close down beside him for a few moments.

"We're going away," she whispered, and there was a curious tremble that was almost a sob in her voice. "We're going home, Kazan. We're going away down where his people live—where they have churches, and cities, and music, and all the beautiful things in the world. And we're going to take *you*, Kazan!"

Kazan didn't understand. But he was happy at having the woman so near to him, and talking to him. At these times he forgot Gray Wolf. The dog that was in him surged over his quarter-strain of wildness, and the woman and the baby alone filled his world. But after Joan had gone to her bed, and all was quiet in the cabin, his old uneasiness returned. He rose to his feet and moved stealthily about the cabin, sniffing at the walls, the door and the things his mistress had done into packages. A low whine rose in his throat. Joan, half asleep, heard it, and murmured: "Be quiet, Kazan. Go to sleep—go to sleep—"

Long after that, Kazan stood rigid in the center of the room, listening, trembling. And faintly he heard, far away, the wailing cry of, Gray Wolf. But to-night it was not the cry of loneliness. It sent a thrill through him. He ran to the door, and whined, but Joan was deep in slumber and did not hear him. Once more he heard the cry, and only once. Then the night grew still. He crouched down near the door.

Joan found him there, still watchful, still listening, when she awoke in the early morning. She came to open the door for him, and in a moment he was gone. His feet seemed scarcely to touch the earth as he sped in the direction of the Sun Rock. Across the plain he could see the cap of it already painted with a golden glow.

He came to the narrow winding trail, and wormed his way up it swiftly.

Gray Wolf was not at the top to greet him. But he could smell her, and the scent of that other thing was strong in the air. His muscles tightened; his legs grew tense. Deep down in his chest there began the low rumble of a growl. He knew now what that strange thing was that had haunted him, and made him uneasy. It was *life*. Something that lived and breathed had invaded the home which he and Gray Wolf had chosen. He bared his long fangs, and a snarl of defiance drew back his lips. Stiff-legged, prepared to spring, his neck and head reaching out, he approached the two rocks between which Gray Wolf had crept the night before. She was still there. And with her was *something else*. After a moment the tenseness left Kazan's body. His bristling crest drooped until it lay flat. His ears shot forward, and he put his head and shoulders between the two rocks, and whined softly. And Gray Wolf whined. Slowly Kazan backed out, and faced the rising sun. Then he lay down, so that his body shielded I the entrance to the chamber between the rocks.

Gray Wolf was a mother.

IX

The Tragedy on Sun Rock

All that day Kazan guarded the top of the Sun Rock. Fate, and the fear and brutality of masters, had heretofore kept him from fatherhood, and he was puzzled. Something told him now that he belonged to the Sun Rock, and not to the cabin. The call that came to him from over the plain was not so strong. At dusk Gray Wolf came out from her retreat, and slunk to his side, whimpering, and nipped gently at his shaggy neck. It was the old instinct of his fathers that made him respond by caressing Gray Wolf's face with his tongue. Then Gray Wolf's jaws opened, and she laughed in short panting breaths, as if she had been hard run. She was happy, and as they heard a little snuffling sound from between the rocks, Kazan wagged his tail, and Gray Wolf darted back to her young.

The babyish cry and its effect upon Gray Wolf taught Kazan his first lesson in fatherhood. Instinct again told him that Gray Wolf could not go down to the hunt with him now—that she must stay at the top of the Sun Rock. So when the moon rose he went down alone, and toward dawn returned with a big white rabbit between his jaws. It was the wild in him that made him do this, and Gray Wolf ate ravenously. Then he knew that each night hereafter he must hunt for Gray Wolf—and the little whimpering creatures hidden between the two rocks.

The next day, and still the next, he did not go to the cabin, though he heard the voices of both the man and the woman calling him. On the fifth he went down, and Joan and the baby were so glad that the woman hugged him, and the baby kicked and laughed and screamed at him, while the man stood by cautiously, watching their demonstrations with a gleam of disapprobation in his eyes.

"I'm afraid of him," he told Joan for the hundredth time. "That's the wolf-gleam in his eyes. He's of a treacherous breed. Sometimes I wish we'd never brought him home."

"If we hadn't—where would the baby—have gone?" Joan reminded him, a little catch in her voice.

"I had almost forgotten that," said her husband. "Kazan, you old devil, I guess I love you, too." He laid his hand caressingly on Kazan's head. "Wonder how he'll take to life down there?" he asked. "He has always been used to the forests. It'll seem mighty strange."

"And so—have I—always been used to the forests," whispered Joan. "I guess that's why I love Kazan—next to you and the baby. Kazan—dear old Kazan!"

This time Kazan felt and scented more of that mysterious change in the cabin. Joan and her husband talked incessantly of their plans when they were together; and when the man was away Joan talked to the baby, and to him. And each time that he came down to the cabin during the week that followed, he grew more and more restless, until at last the man noticed the change in him.

"I believe he knows," he said to Joan one evening. "I believe he knows we're preparing to leave." Then he added: "The river was rising again to-day. It will be another week before we can start, perhaps longer."

That same night the moon flooded the top of the Sun Rock with a golden light, and out into the glow of it came Gray Wolf, with her three little whelps toddling behind her. There was much about these soft little balls that tumbled about him and snuggled in his tawny coat that reminded Kazan of the baby. At times they made the same queer, soft little sounds, and they staggered about on their four little legs just as helplessly as baby Joan made her way about on two. He did not fondle them, as Gray Wolf did, but the touch of them, and their babyish whimperings, filled him with a kind of pleasure that he had never experienced before.

The moon was straight above them, and the night was almost as bright as day, when he went down again to hunt for Gray Wolf. At the foot of the rock a big white rabbit popped up ahead of him, and he gave chase. For half a mile he pursued, until the wolf instinct in him rose over the dog, and he gave up the futile race. A deer he might have overtaken, but small game the wolf must hunt as the fox hunts it, and he began to slip through the thickets slowly and as quietly as a shadow. He was a mile from the Sun Rock when two quick leaps put Gray Wolf's supper between his jaws. He trotted back slowly, dropping the big seven-pound snow-shoe hare now and then to rest.

When he came to the narrow trail that led to the top of the Sun Rock he stopped. In that trail was the warm scent of strange feet. The rabbit fell from his jaws. Every hair in his body was suddenly electrified into life. What he scented was not the scent of a rabbit, a marten or a porcupine. Fang and claw had climbed the path ahead of him. And then, coming faintly to him from the top of the rock, he heard sounds which sent him up with a terrible whining cry. When he reached the summit he saw in the white moonlight a scene that stopped him for a single moment. Close to the edge of the sheer fall to the rocks, fifty feet below, Gray Wolf was engaged in a death-struggle with a huge gray lynx. She was down—and under, and from her there came a sudden sharp terrible cry of pain.

Kazan flew across the rock. His attack was the swift silent assault of the wolf, combined with the greater courage, the fury and the strategy of the husky. Another husky would have died in that first attack. But the lynx was not a dog or a wolf. It was "Mow-lee, the swift," as the Sarcees had named it—the quickest creature in the wilderness. Kazan's inch-long fangs should have sunk deep in its jugular. But in a fractional part of a second the lynx had thrown itself back like a huge soft ball, and Kazan's teeth buried themselves in the flesh of its neck instead of the jugular. And Kazan was not now fighting the fangs of a wolf in the pack, or of another husky. He was fighting claws—claws that ripped like twenty razor-edged knives, and which even a jugular hold could not stop.

Once he had fought a lynx in a trap, and he had not forgotten the lesson the battle had taught him. He fought to pull the lynx *down*, instead of forcing it on its back, as he would have done with another dog or a wolf. He knew that when on its back the fierce cat was most dangerous. One rip of its powerful hindfeet could disembowel him.

Behind him he heard Gray Wolf sobbing and crying, and he knew that she was terribly hurt. He was filled with the rage and strength of two dogs, and his teeth met through the flesh and hide of the cat's throat. But the big lynx escaped death by half an inch. It would take a fresh grip to reach the jugular, and suddenly Kazan made the deadly lunge. There was an instant's freedom for the lynx, and in that moment it flung itself back, and Kazan gripped at its throat—*on top*.

The cat's claws ripped through his flesh, cutting open his side—a little too high to kill. Another stroke and they would have cut to his vitals. But they had struggled close to the edge of the rock wall, and suddenly, without a snarl or a cry, they rolled over. It was fifty or sixty feet to the rocks of the ledge below, and even as they pitched over and over in the fall, Kazan's teeth sank deeper. They struck with terrific force, Kazan uppermost. The shock sent him half a dozen feet from his enemy. He was up like a flash, dizzy, snarling, on the defensive. The lynx lay limp and motionless where it had fallen. Kazan came nearer, still prepared, and sniffed cautiously. Something told him that the fight was over. He turned and dragged himself slowly along the ledge to the trail, and returned to Gray Wolf.

Gray Wolf was no longer in the moonlight. Close to the two rocks lay the limp and lifeless little bodies of the three pups. The lynx had torn them to pieces. With a whine of grief Kazan approached the two boulders and thrust his head between them. Gray Wolf was there, crying to herself in that terrible sobbing way. He went in, and began to lick her bleeding shoulders and head. All the rest of that night she whimpered with pain. With dawn she dragged herself out to the lifeless little bodies on the rock.

And then Kazan saw the terrible work of the lynx. For Gray Wolf was blind—not for a day or a night, but blind for all time. A gloom that no sun could break had become her shroud. And perhaps again it was that instinct of animal creation, which often is more wonderful than man's reason, that told Kazan what had happened. For he knew now that she was helpless—more helpless than the little creatures that had gamboled in the moonlight a few hours before. He remained close beside her all that day.

Vainly that day did Joan call for Kazan. Her voice rose to the Sun Rock, and Gray Wolf's head snuggled closer to Kazan, and Kazan's ears dropped back, and he licked her wounds. Late in the afternoon Kazan left Gray Wolf long enough to run to the bottom of the trail and bring up the snow-shoe rabbit. Gray Wolf muzzled the fur and flesh, but would not eat. Still a little later Kazan urged her to follow him to the trail. He no longer wanted to stay at the top of the Sun Rock, and he no longer wanted Gray Wolf to stay there. Step by step he drew her down the winding path away from her dead puppies. She would move only when he was very near her—so near that she could touch his scarred flank with her nose.

They came at last to the point in the trail where they had to leap down a distance of three or four feet from the edge of a rock, and here Kazan saw how utterly helpless Gray Wolf had become. She whined, and crouched twenty times before she dared make the spring, and then she jumped stiff-legged, and fell in a heap at Kazan's feet. After this Kazan did not have to urge her so hard, for the fall impinged on her the fact that she was safe only when her muzzle touched her mate's flank. She followed him obediently when they reached the plain, trotting with her foreshoulder to his hip.

Kazan was heading for a thicket in the creek bottom half a mile away, and a dozen times in that short distance Gray Wolf stumbled and fell. And each time that she fell Kazan learned a little more of the limitations of blindness. Once he sprang off in pursuit of a rabbit, but he had not taken twenty leaps when he stopped and looked back. Gray Wolf had not moved an inch. She stood motionless, sniffing the air—waiting for him! For a full minute Kazan stood, also waiting. Then he returned to her. Ever after this he returned to the point where he had left Gray Wolf, knowing that he would find her there.

All that day they remained in the thicket. In the afternoon he visited the cabin. Joan and her husband were there, and both saw at once Kazan's torn side and his lacerated head and shoulders.

"Pretty near a finish fight for him," said the man, after he had examined him. "It was either a lynx or a bear. Another wolf could not do that."

For half an hour Joan worked over him, talking to him all the time, and fondling him with her soft hands. She bathed his wounds in warm water, and then covered them with a healing salve, and Kazan was filled again with that old restful desire to remain with her always, and never to go back into the forests. For an hour she let him lie on the edge of her dress, with his nose touching her foot, while she worked on baby things. Then she rose to prepare supper, and Kazan got up—a little wearily—and went to the door. Gray Wolf and the gloom of the night were calling him, and he answered that call with a slouch of his shoulders and a drooping head. Its old thrill was gone. He watched his chance, and went out through the door. The moon had risen when he rejoined Gray Wolf. She greeted his return with a low whine of joy, and muzzled him with her blind face. In her helplessness she looked happier than Kazan in all his strength.

From now on, during the days that followed, it was a last great fight between blind and faithful Gray Wolf and the woman. If Joan had known of what lay in the thicket, if she could once have seen the poor creature to whom Kazan was now all life—the sun, the stars, the moon, and food—she would have helped Gray Wolf. But as it was she tried to lure Kazan more and more to the cabin, and slowly she won.

At last the great day came, eight days after the fight on the Sun Rock. Kazan had taken Gray Wolf to a wooded point on the river two days before, and there he had left her the preceding night when he went to the cabin. This time a stout babiche thong was tied to the collar round his neck, and he was fastened to a staple in the log wall. Joan and her husband were up before it was light next day. The sun was just rising when they all went out, the man carrying the baby, and Joan leading him. Joan turned and locked the cabin door, and Kazan heard a sob in her throat as they followed the man down to the river. The big canoe was packed and waiting. Joan got in first, with the baby. Then, still holding the babiche thong, she drew Kazan up close to her, so that he lay with his weight against her.

The sun fell warmly on Kazan's back as they shoved off, and he closed his eyes, and rested his head on Joan's lap. Her hand fell softly on his shoulder. He heard again that sound which the man could not hear, the broken sob in her throat, as the canoe moved slowly down to the wooded point.

Joan waved her hand back at the cabin, just disappearing behind the trees.

"Good-by!" she cried sadly. "Good-by—" And then she buried her face close down to Kazan and the baby, and sobbed.

The man stopped paddling.

"You're not sorry—Joan?" he asked.

They were drifting past the point now, and the scent of Gray Wolf came to Kazan's nostrils, rousing him, and bringing a low whine from his throat.

"You're not sorry—we're going?" Joan shook her head.

"No," she replied. "Only I've—always lived here—in the forests— and they're—home!"

The point with its white finger of sand, was behind them now. And Kazan was standing rigid, facing it. The man called to him, and Joan lifted her head. She, too, saw the point, and suddenly the babiche leash slipped from her fingers, and a strange light leaped into her blue eyes as she saw what stood at the end of that white tip of sand. It was Gray Wolf. Her blind eyes were turned toward Kazan. At last Gray Wolf, the faithful, understood. Scent told her what her eyes could not see. Kazan and the man-smell were together. And they were going—going— going—

"Look!" whispered Joan.

The man turned. Gray Wolf's forefeet were in the water. And now, as the canoe drifted farther and farther away, she settled back on her haunches, raised her head to the sun which she could not see and gave her last long wailing cry for Kazan.

The canoe lurched. A tawny body shot through the air—and Kazan was gone.

The man reached forward for his rifle. Joan's hand stopped him. Her face was white.

"Let him go back to her! Let him go—let him go!" she cried. "It is his place—with her."

And Kazan reaching the shore, shook the water from his shaggy hair, and looked for the last time toward the woman. The canoe was drifting slowly around the first bend. A moment more and it had disappeared. Gray Wolf had won.

X

The Days of Fire

From the night of the terrible fight with the big gray lynx on the top of the Sun Rock, Kazan remembered less and less vividly the old days when he had been a sledge-dog, and the leader of a pack. He would never quite forget them, and always there would stand out certain memories from among the rest, like fires cutting the blackness of night. But as man dates events from his birth, his marriage, his freedom from a bondage, or some foundation-step in his career, so all things seemed to Kazan to begin with two tragedies which had followed one fast upon the other after the birth of Gray Wolf's pups.

The first was the fight on the Sun Rock, when the big gray lynx had blinded his beautiful wolf mate for all time, and had torn her pups into pieces. He in turn had killed the lynx. But Gray Wolf was still blind. Vengeance had not been able to give her sight. She could no longer hunt with him, as they had hunted with the wild wolf-packs out on the plain, and in the dark forests. So at thought of that night he always snarled, and his lips curled back to reveal his inch-long fangs.

The other tragedy was the going of Joan, her baby and her husband. Something more infallible than reason told Kazan that they would not come back. Brightest of all the pictures that remained with him was that of the sunny morning when the woman and the baby he loved, and the man he endured because of them, had gone away in the canoe, and often he would go to the point, and gaze longingly down-stream, where he had leaped from the canoe to return to his blind mate.

So Kazan's life seemed now to be made up chiefly of three things: his hatred of everything that bore the scent or mark of the lynx, his grieving for Joan and the baby, and Gray Wolf. It was natural that the strongest passion in him should be his hatred of the lynx, for not only Gray Wolf's blindness and the death of the pups, but even the loss of the woman and the baby he laid to that fatal struggle on the Sun Rock. From that hour he became the deadliest enemy of the lynx tribe. Wherever he struck the scent of the big gray cat he was turned into a snarling demon, and his hatred grew day by day, as he became more completely a part of the wild.

He found that Gray Wolf was more necessary to him now than she had ever been since the day she had left the wolf-pack for him. He was three-quarters dog, and the dog-part of him demanded companionship. There was only Gray Wolf to give him that now. They were alone. Civilization was four hundred miles south of them. The nearest Hudson's Bay post was sixty miles to the west. Often, in the days of the woman and the baby, Gray Wolf had spent her nights alone out in the forest, waiting and calling for Kazan. Now it was Kazan who was lonely and uneasy when he was away from her side.

In her blindness Gray Wolf could no longer hunt with her mate. But gradually a new code of understanding grew up between them, and through her blindness they learned many things that they had not known before. By early summer Gray Wolf could travel with Kazan, if he did not move too swiftly. She ran at his flank, with her shoulder or muzzle touching him, and Kazan learned not to leap, but to trot. Very quickly he found that he must choose the easiest trails for Gray Wolf's feet. When they came to a space to be bridged by a leap, he would muzzle Gray Wolf and whine, and she would stand with ears alert—listening. Then Kazan would take the leap, and she understood the distance she had to cover. She always over-leaped, which was a good fault.

In another way, and one that was destined to serve them many times in the future, she became of greater help than ever to Kazan. Scent and hearing entirely took the place of sight. Each day developed these senses more and more, and at the same time there developed between them the dumb language whereby she could impress upon Kazan what she had discovered by scent or sound. It became a curious habit of Kazan's always to look at Gray Wolf when they stopped to listen, or to scent the air.

After the fight on the Sun Rock, Kazan had taken his blind mate to a thick clump of spruce and balsam in the river-bottom, where they remained until early summer. Every day for weeks Kazan went to the cabin where Joan and the baby—and the man—had been. For a long time he went hopefully, looking each day or night to see some sign of life there. But the door was never open. The boards and saplings at the windows always remained. Never a spiral of smoke rose from the clay chimney. Grass and vines began to grow in the path. And fainter and fainter grew that scent which Kazan could still find about it—the scent of man, of the woman, the baby.

One day he found a little baby moccasin under one of the closed windows. It was old, and worn out, and blackened by snow and rain, but he lay down beside it, and remained there for a long time, while the baby Joan—a thousand miles away—was playing with the strange toys of civilization. Then he returned to Gray Wolf among the spruce and balsam.

The cabin was the one place to which Gray Wolf would not follow him. At all other times she was at his side. Now that she had become accustomed to blindness, she even accompanied him on his hunts, until he struck game, and began the chase. Then she would wait for him. Kazan usually hunted the big snow-shoe rabbits. But one night he ran down and killed a young doe. The kill was too heavy to drag to Gray Wolf, so he returned to where she was waiting for him and guided her to the feast. In many ways they became more and more inseparable as the summer lengthened, until at last, through all the wilderness, their footprints were always two by two and never one by one.

Then came the great fire.

Gray Wolf caught the scent of it when it was still two days to the west. The sun that night went down in a lurid cloud. The moon, drifting into the west, became blood red. When it dropped behind the wilderness in this manner, the Indians called it the Bleeding Moon, and the air was filled with omens.

All the next day Gray Wolf was nervous, and toward noon Kazan caught in the air the warning that she had sensed many hours ahead of him. Steadily the scent grew stronger, and by the middle of the afternoon the sun was veiled by a film of smoke.

The flight of the wild things from the triangle of forest between the junctions of the Pipestone and Cree Rivers would have begun then, but the wind shifted. It was a fatal shift. The fire was raging from the west and south. Then the wind swept straight eastward, carrying the smoke with it, and during this breathing spell all the wild creatures in the triangle between the two rivers waited. This gave the fire time to sweep completely, across the base of the forest triangle, cutting off the last trails of escape.

Then the wind shifted again, and the fire swept north. The head of the triangle became a death-trap. All through the night the southern sky was filled with a lurid glow, and by morning the heat and smoke and ash were suffocating.

Panic-striken, Kazan searched vainly for a means of escape. Not for an instant did he leave Gray Wolf. It would have been easy for him to swim across either of the two streams, for he was three-quarters dog. But at the first touch of water on her paws, Gray Wolf drew back, shrinking. Like all her breed, she would face fire and death before water. Kazan urged. A dozen times he leaped in, and swam out into the stream. But Gray Wolf would come no farther than she could wade.

They could hear the distant murmuring roar of the fire now. Ahead of it came the wild things. Moose, caribou and deer plunged into the water of the streams and swam to the safety of the opposite side. Out upon a white finger of sand lumbered a big black bear with two cubs, and even the cubs took to the water, and swam across easily. Kazan watched them, and whined to Gray Wolf.

And then out upon that white finger of sand came other things that dreaded the water as Gray Wolf dreaded it: a big fat porcupine, a sleek little marten, a fisher-cat that sniffed the air and wailed like a child. Those things that could not or would not swim outnumbered the others three to one. Hundreds of little ermine scurried along the shore like rats, their squeaking little voices sounding incessantly; foxes ran swiftly along the banks, seeking a tree or a windfall that might bridge the water for them; the lynx snarled and faced the fire; and Gray Wolf's own tribe—the wolves—dared take no deeper step than she.

Dripping and panting, and half choked by heat and smoke, Kazan came to Gray Wolf's side. There was but one refuge left near them, and that was the sand-bar. It reached out for fifty feet into the stream. Quickly he led his blind mate toward it. As they came through the low bush to the river-bed, something stopped them both. To their nostrils had come the scent of a deadlier enemy than fire. A lynx had taken possession of the sand-bar, and was crouching at the end of it. Three porcupines had dragged themselves into the edge of the water, and lay there like balls, their quills alert and quivering. A fisher-cat was snarling at the lynx. And the lynx, with ears laid back, watched Kazan and Gray Wolf as they began the invasion of the sand-bar.

Faithful Gray Wolf was full of fight, and she sprang shoulder to shoulder with Kazan, her fangs bared. With an angry snap, Kazan drove her back, and she stood quivering and whining while he advanced. Light-footed, his pointed ears forward, no menace or threat in his attitude, he advanced. It was the deadly advance of the husky trained in battle, skilled in the art of killing. A man from civilization would have said that the dog was approaching the lynx with friendly intentions. But the lynx understood. It was the old feud of many generations—made deadlier now by Kazan's memory of that night at the top of the Sun Rock.

Instinct told the fisher-cat what was coming, and it crouched low and flat; the porcupines, scolding like little children at the presence of enemies and the thickening clouds of smoke, thrust their quills still more erect. The lynx lay on its belly, like a cat, its hindquarters twitching, and gathered for the spring. Kazan's feet seemed scarcely to touch the sand as he circled lightly around it. The lynx pivoted as he circled, and then it shot in a round snarling ball over the eight feet of space that separated them.

Kazan did not leap aside. He made no effort to escape the attack, but met it fairly with the full force of his shoulders, as sledge-dog meets sledge-dog. He was ten pounds heavier than the lynx, and for a moment the big loose-jointed cat with its twenty knife-like claws was thrown on its side. Like a flash Kazan took advantage of the moment, and drove for the back of the cat's neck.

In that same moment blind Gray Wolf leaped in with a snarling cry, and fighting under Kazan's belly, she fastened her jaws in one of the cat's hindlegs. The bone snapped. The lynx, twice outweighed, leaped backward, dragging both Kazan and Gray Wolf. It fell back down on one of the porcupines, and a hundred quills drove into its body. Another leap and it was free—fleeing into the face of the smoke. Kazan did not pursue. Gray Wolf came to his side and licked his neck, where fresh blood was crimsoning his tawny hide. The fisher-cat lay as if dead, watching them with fierce little black eyes. The porcupines continued to chatter, as if begging for mercy. And then a thick black suffocating pall of smoke drove low over the sand-bar and with it came air that was furnace-hot.

At the uttermost end of the sand-bar Kazan and Gray Wolf rolled themselves into balls and thrust their heads under their bodies. The fire was very near now. The roar of it was like that of a great cataract, with now and then a louder crash of falling trees. The air was filled with ash and burning sparks, and twice Kazan drew forth his head to snap at blazing embers that fell upon and seared him like hot irons.

Close along the edge of the stream grew thick green bush, and when the fire reached this, it burned more slowly, and the heat grew less. Still, it was a long time before Kazan and Gray Wolf could draw forth their heads and breathe more freely. Then they found that the finger of sand reaching out into the river had saved them. Everywhere in that triangle between the two rivers the world had turned black, and was hot underfoot.

The smoke cleared away. The wind changed again, and swung down cool and fresh from the west and north. The fisher-cat was the first to move cautiously back to the forests that had been, but the porcupines were still rolled into balls when Gray Wolf and Kazan left the sand-bar. They began to travel up-stream, and before night came, their feet were sore from hot ash and burning embers.

The moon was strange and foreboding that night, like a spatter of blood in the sky, and through the long silent hours there was not even the hoot of an owl to give a sign that life still existed where yesterday had been a paradise of wild things. Kazan knew that there was nothing to hunt, and they continued to travel all that night. With dawn they struck a narrow swamp along the edge of the stream. Here beavers had built a dam, and they were able to cross over into the green country on the opposite side. For another day and another night they traveled westward, and this brought them into the thick country of swamp and timber along the Waterfound.

And as Kazan and Gray Wolf came from the west, there came from the Hudson's Bay post to the east a slim dark-faced French half-breed by the name of Henri Loti, the most famous lynx hunter in all the Hudson's Bay country. He was prospecting for "signs," and he found them in abundance along the Waterfound. It was a game paradise, and the snow-shoe rabbit abounded in thousands. As a consequence, the lynxes were thick, and Henri built his trapping shack, and then returned to the post to wait until the first snows fell, when he would come back with his team, supplies and traps.

And up from the south, at this same time, there was slowly working his way by canoe and trail a young university zoologist who was gathering material for a book on *The Reasoning of the Wild*. His name was Paul Weyman, and he had made arrangements to spend a part of the winter with Henri Loti, the half-breed. He brought with him plenty of paper, a camera and the photograph of a girl. His only weapon was a pocket-knife.

And meanwhile Kazan and Gray Wolf found the home they were seeking in a thick swamp five or six miles from the cabin that Henri Loti had built.

XI

Always Two by Two

It was January when a guide from the post brought Paul Weyman to Henri Loti's cabin on the Waterfound. He was a man of thirty-two or three, full of the red-blooded life that made Henri like him at once. If this had not been the case, the first few days in the cabin might have been unpleasant, for Henri was in bad humor. He told Weyman about it their first night, as they were smoking pipes alongside the redly glowing box stove.

"It is damn strange," said Henri. "I have lost seven lynx in the traps, torn to pieces like they were no more than rabbits that the foxes had killed. No thing—not even bear—have ever tackled lynx in a trap before. It is the first time I ever see it. And they are torn up so bad they are not worth one half dollar at the post. Seven!—that is over two hundred dollar I have lost! There are two wolves who do it. Two—I know it by the tracks—always two—an'—never one. They follow my trap-line an' eat the rabbits I catch. They leave the fisher-cat, an' the mink, an' the ermine, an' the marten; but the lynx—*sacré* an' damn!—they jump on him an' pull the fur from him like you pull the wild cotton balls from the burn-bush! I have tried strychnine in deer fat, an' I have set traps and deadfalls, but I can not catch them. They will drive me out unless I get them, for I have taken only five good lynx, an' they have destroyed seven."

This roused Weyman. He was one of that growing number of thoughtful men who believe that man's egoism, as a race, blinds him to many of the more wonderful facts of creation. He had thrown down the gantlet, and with a logic that had gained him a nation-wide hearing, to those who believed that man was the only living creature who could reason, and that common sense and cleverness when displayed by any other breathing thing were merely instinct. The facts behind Henri's tale of woe struck him as important, and until midnight they talked about the two strange wolves.

"There is one big wolf an' one smaller," said Henri. "An' it is always the big wolf who goes in an' fights the lynx. I see that by the snow. While he's fighting, the smaller wolf makes many tracks in the snow just out of reach, an' then when the lynx is down, or dead, it jumps in an' helps tear it into pieces. All that I know by the snow. Only once have I seen where the smaller one went in an' fought with the other, an' then there was blood all about that was not lynx blood; I trailed the devils a mile by the dripping."

During the two weeks that followed, Weyman found much to add to the material of his book. Not a day passed that somewhere along Henri's trap-line they did not see the trails of the two wolves, and Weyman observed that—as Henri had told him—the footprints were always two by two, and never one by one. On the third day they came to a trap that had held a lynx, and at sight of what remained Henri cursed in both French and English until he was purple in the face. The lynx had been torn until its pelt was practically worthless.

Weyman saw where the smaller wolf had waited on its haunches, while its companion had killed the lynx. He did not tell Henri all he thought. But the days that followed convinced him more and more that he had found the most dramatic exemplification of his theory. Back of this mysterious tragedy of the trap-line there was a *reason*.

Why did the two wolves not destroy the fisher-cat, the ermine and the marten? Why was their feud with the lynx alone?

Weyman was strangely thrilled. He was a lover of wild things, and for that reason he never carried a gun. And when he saw Henri placing poison-baits for the two marauders, he shuddered, and when, day after day, he saw that these poison-baits were untouched, he rejoiced. Something in his own nature went out in sympathy to the heroic outlaw of the trap-line who never failed to give battle to the lynx. Nights in the cabin he wrote down his thoughts and discoveries of the day. One night he turned suddenly on Henri.

"Henri, doesn't it ever make you sorry to kill so many wild things?" he asked.

Henri stared and shook his head.

"I kill t'ousand an' t'ousand," he said. "I kill t'ousand more."

"And there are twenty thousand others just like you in this northern quarter of the continent—all killing, killing for hundreds of years back, and yet you can't kill out wild life. The war of Man and the Beast, you might call it. And, if you could return five hundred years from now, Henri, you'd still find wild life here. Nearly all the rest of the world is changing, but you can't change these almost impenetrable thousands of square miles of ridges and swamps and forests. The railroads won't come here, and I, for one, thank God for that. Take all the great prairies to the west, for instance. Why, the old buffalo trails are still there, plain as day—and yet, towns and cities are growing up everywhere. Did you ever hear of North Battleford?"

"Is she near Montreal or Quebec?" Henri asked.

Weyman smiled, and drew a photograph from his pocket. It was the picture of a girl.

"No. It's far to the west, in Saskatchewan. Seven years ago I used to go up there every year, to shoot prairie chickens, coyotes and elk. There wasn't any North Battleford then—just the glorious prairie, hundreds and hundreds of square miles of it. There was a single shack on the Saskatchewan River, where North Battleford now stands, and I used to stay there. In that shack there was a little girl, twelve years old. We used to go out hunting together—for I used to kill things in those days. And the little girl would cry sometimes when I killed, and I'd laugh at her.

"Then a railroad came, and then another, and they joined near the shack, and all at once a town sprang up. Seven years ago there was only the shack there, Henri. Two years ago there were eighteen hundred people. This year, when I came through, there were five thousand, and two years from now there'll be ten thousand.

"On the ground where that shack stood are three banks, with a capital of forty million dollars; you can see the glow of the electric lights of the city twenty miles away. It has a hundred-thousand dollar college, a high school, the provincial asylum, a fire department, two clubs, a board of trade, and it's going to have a street-car line within two years. Think of that—all where the coyotes howled a few years ago!

"People are coming in so fast that they can't keep a census. Five years from now there'll be a city of twenty thousand where the old shack stood. And the little girl in that shack, Henri—she's a young lady now, and her people are—well, rich. I don't care about that. The chief thing is that she is going to marry me in the spring. Because of her I stopped killing things when she was only sixteen. The last thing I killed was a prairie wolf, and it had young. Eileen kept the little puppy. She's got it now—tamed. That's why above all other wild things I love the wolves. And I hope these two leave your trap-line safe."

Henri was staring at him. Weyman gave him the picture. It was of a sweet-faced girl, with deep pure eyes, and there came a twitch at the corners of Henri's mouth as he looked at it.

"My Iowaka died t'ree year ago," he said. "She too loved the wild thing. But them wolf—damn! They drive me out if I can not kill them!" He put fresh fuel into the stove, and prepared for bed.

One day the big idea came to Henri.

Weyman was with him when they struck fresh signs of lynx. There was a great windfall ten or fifteen feet high, and in one place the logs had formed a sort of cavern, with almost solid walls on three sides. The snow was beaten down by tracks, and the fur of rabbit was scattered about. Henri was jubilant.

"We got heem—sure!" he said.

He built the bait-house, set a trap and looked about him shrewdly. Then he explained his scheme to Weyman. If the lynx was caught, and the two wolves came to destroy it, the fight would take place in that shelter under the windfall, and the marauders would have to pass through the opening. So Henri set five smaller traps, concealing them skilfully under leaves and moss and snow, and all were far enough away from the bait-house so that the trapped lynx could not spring them in his struggles.

"When they fight, wolf jump this way an' that—an' sure get in," said Henri. "He miss one, two, t'ree—but he sure get in trap somewhere."

That same morning a light snow fell, making the work more complete, for it covered up all footprints and buried the telltale scent of man. That night Kazan and Gray Wolf passed within a hundred feet of the windfall, and Gray Wolf's keen scent detected something strange and disquieting in the air. She informed Kazan by pressing her shoulder against his, and they swung off at right angles, keeping to windward of the trap-line.

For two days and three cold starlit nights nothing happened at the windfall. Henri understood, and explained to Weyman. The lynx was a hunter, like himself, and also had its hunt-line, which it covered about once a week. On the fifth night the lynx returned, went to the windfall, was lured straight to the bait, and the sharp-toothed steel trap closed relentlessly over its right hindfoot. Kazan and Gray Wolf were traveling a quarter of a mile deeper in the forest when they heard the clanking of the steel chain as the lynx fought; to free itself. Ten minutes later they stood in the door of the windfall cavern.

It was a white clear night, so filled with brilliant stars that Henri himself could have hunted by the light of them. The lynx had exhausted itself, and lay crouching on its belly as Kazan and Gray Wolf appeared.

As usual, Gray Wolf held back while Kazan began the battle. In the first or second of these fights on the trap-line, Kazan would probably have been disemboweled or had his jugular vein cut open, had the fierce cats been free. They were more than his match in open fight, though the biggest of them fell ten pounds under his weight. Chance had saved him on the Sun Rock. Gray Wolf and the porcupine had both added to the defeat of the lynx on the sand-bar. And along Henri's hunting line it was the trap that was his ally. Even with his enemy thus shackled he took big chances. And he took bigger chances than ever with the lynx under the windfall.

The cat was an old warrior, six or seven years old. His claws were an inch and a quarter long, and curved like simitars. His forefeet and his left hindfoot were free, and as Kazan advanced, he drew back, so that the trap-chain was slack under his body. Here Kazan could not follow his old tactics of circling about his trapped foe, until it had become tangled in the chain, or had so shortened and twisted it that there was no chance for a leap. He had to attack face to face, and suddenly he lunged in. They met shoulder to shoulder. Kazan's fangs snapped at the other's throat, and missed. Before he could strike again, the lynx flung out its free hindfoot, and even Gray Wolf heard the ripping sound that it made. With a snarl Kazan was flung back, his shoulder torn to the bone.

Then it was that one of Henri's hidden traps saved him from a second attack—and death. Steel jaws snapped over one of his forefeet, and when he leaped, the chain stopped him. Once or twice before, blind Gray Wolf had leaped in, when she knew that Kazan was in great danger. For an instant she forgot her caution now, and as she heard Kazan's snarl of pain, she sprang in under the windfall. Five traps Henri had hidden in the space in front of the bait-house, and Gray Wolf's feet found two of these. She fell on her side, snapping and snarling. In his struggles Kazan sprung the remaining two traps. One of them missed. The fifth, and last, caught him by a hindfoot.

This was a little past midnight. From then until morning the earth and snow under the windfall were torn up by the struggles of the wolf, the dog and the lynx to regain their freedom. And when morning came, all three were exhausted, and lay on their sides, panting and with bleeding jaws, waiting for the coming of man—and death.

Henri and Weyman were out early. When they struck off the main line toward the windfall, Henri pointed to the tracks of Kazan and

Gray Wolf, and his dark face lighted up with pleasure and excitement. When they reached the shelter under the mass of fallen timber, both stood speechless for a moment, astounded by what they saw. Even Henri had seen nothing like this before—two wolves and a lynx, all in traps, and almost within reach of one another's fangs. But surprise could not long delay the business of Henri's hunter's instinct. The wolves lay first in his path, and he was raising his rifle to put a steel-capped bullet through the base of Kazan's brain, when Weyman caught him eagerly by the arm. Weyman was staring. His fingers dug into Henri's flesh. His eyes had caught a glimpse of the steel-studded collar about Kazan's neck.

"Wait!" he cried. "It's not a wolf. It's a dog!"

Henri lowered his rifle, staring at the collar. Weyman's eyes shot to Gray Wolf. She was facing them, snarling, her white fangs bared to the foes she could not see. Her blind eyes were closed. Where there should have been eyes there was only hair, and an exclamation broke from Weyman's lips.

"Look!" he commanded of Henri. "What in the name of heaven—"

"One is dog—wild dog that has run to the wolves," said Henri. "And the other is—wolf."

"And *blind*!" gasped Weyman.

"*Oui*, blind, m'sieur," added Henri, falling partly into French in his amazement. He was raising his rifle again. Weyman seized it firmly.

"Don't kill them, Henri," he said. "Give them to me—alive. Figure up the value of the lynx they have destroyed, and add to that the wolf bounty, and I will pay. Alive, they are worth to me a great deal. My God, a dog—and a blind wolf—*mates*!"

He still held Henri's rifle, and Henri was staring at him, as if he did not yet quite understand.

Weyman continued speaking, his eyes and face blazing.

"A dog—and a blind wolf—*mates*!" he repeated. "It is wonderful, Henri. Down there, they will say I have gone beyond *reason*, when my book comes out. But I shall have proof. I shall take twenty photographs here, before you kill the lynx. I shall keep the dog and the wolf alive. And I shall pay you, Henri, a hundred dollars apiece for the two. May I have them?"

Henri nodded. He held his rifle in readiness, while Weyman unpacked his camera and got to work. Snarling fangs greeted the click of the camera-shutter—the fangs of wolf and lynx. But Kazan lay cringing, not through fear, but because he still recognized the mastery of man. And when he had finished with his pictures, Weyman approached almost within reach of him, and spoke even more kindly to him than the man who had lived back in the deserted cabin.

Henri shot the lynx, and when Kazan understood this, he tore at the end of his trap-chains and snarled at the writhing body of his forest enemy. By means of a pole and a babiche noose, Kazan was brought out from under the windfall and taken to Henri's cabin. The two men then returned with a thick sack and more babiche, and blind Gray Wolf, still fettered by the traps, was made prisoner. All the rest of that day Weyman and Henri worked to build a stout cage of saplings, and when it was finished, the two prisoners were placed in it.

Before the dog was put in with Gray Wolf, Weyman closely examined the worn and tooth-marked collar about his neck.

On the brass plate he found engraved the one word, "Kazan," and with a strange thrill made note of it in his diary.

After this Weyman often remained at the cabin when Henri went out on the trap-line. After the second day he dared to put his hand between the sapling bars and touch Kazan, and the next day Kazan accepted a piece of raw moose meat from his hand. But at his approach, Gray Wolf would always hide under the pile of balsam in the corner of their prison. The instinct of generations and perhaps of centuries had taught her that man was her deadliest enemy. And yet, this man did not hurt her, and Kazan was not afraid of him. She was frightened at first; then puzzled, and a growing curiosity followed that. Occasionally, after the third day, she would thrust her blind face out of the balsam and sniff the air when Weyman was at the cage, making friends with Kazan. But she would not eat. Weyman noted that, and each day he tempted her with the choicest morsels of deer and moose fat. Five days—six—seven passed, and she had not taken a mouthful. Weyman could count her ribs.

"She die," Henri told him on the seventh night. "She starve before she eat in that cage. She want the forest, the wild kill, the fresh blood. She two—t'ree year old—too old to make civilize."

Henri went to bed at the usual hour, but Weyman was troubled, and sat up late. He wrote a long letter to the sweet-faced girl at North Battleford, and then he turned out the light, and painted visions of her in the red glow of the fire. He saw her again for that first time when he camped in the little shack where the fifth city of Saskatchewan now stood—with her blue eyes, the big shining braid, and the fresh glow of the prairies in her cheeks. She had hated him—yes, actually hated him, because he loved to kill. He laughed softly as he thought of that. She had changed him—wonderfully.

He rose, opened the door, softly, and went out. Instinctively his eyes turned westward. The sky was a blaze of stars. In their light he could see the cage, and he stood, watching and listening. A sound came to him. It was Gray Wolf gnawing at the sapling bars of her prison. A moment later there came a low sobbing whine, and he knew that it was Kazan crying for his freedom.

Leaning against the side of the cabin was an ax. Weyman seized it, and his lips smiled silently. He was thrilled by a strange happiness, and a thousand miles away in that city on the Saskatchewan he could feel another spirit rejoicing with him. He moved toward the cage. A dozen blows, and two of the sapling bars were knocked out. Then Weyman drew back. Gray Wolf found the opening first, and she slipped out into the starlight like a shadow. But she did not flee. Out in the open space she waited for Kazan, and for a moment the two stood there, looking at the cabin. Then they set off into freedom, Gray Wolf's shoulder at Kazan's flank.

Weyman breathed deeply.

"Two by two—always two by two, until death finds one of them," he whispered.

XII

The Red Death

Kazan and Gray Wolf wandered northward into the Fond du Lac country, and were there when Jacques, a Hudson Bay Company's runner, came up to the post from the south with the first authentic news of the dread plague—the smallpox. For weeks there had been rumors on all sides. And rumor grew into rumor. From the east, the south and the west they multiplied, until on all sides the Paul Reveres of the wilderness were carrying word that *La Mort Rouge*—the Red Death—was at their heels, and the chill of a great fear swept like a shivering wind from the edge of civilization to the bay. Nineteen years before these same rumors had come up from the south, and the Red Terror had followed. The horror of it still remained with the forest people, for a thousand unmarked graves, shunned like a pestilence, and scattered from the lower waters of James Bay to the lake country of the Athabasca, gave evidence of the toll it demanded.

Now and then in their wanderings Kazan and Gray Wolf had come upon the little mounds that covered the dead. Instinct—something that was infinitely beyond the comprehension of man—made them *feel* the presence of death about them, perhaps smell it in the air. Gray Wolf's wild blood and her blindness gave her an immense advantage over Kazan when it came to detecting those mysteries of the air and the earth which the eyes were not made to see. Each day that had followed that terrible moonlit night on the Sun Rock, when the lynx had blinded her, had added to the infallibility of her two chief senses—hearing and scent. And it was she who discovered the presence of the plague first, just as she had scented the great forest fire hours before Kazan had found it in the air.

Kazan had lured her back to a trap-line. The trail they found was old. It had not been traveled for many days. In a trap they found a rabbit, but it had been dead a long time. In another there was the carcass of a fox, torn into bits by the owls. Most of the traps were sprung. Others were covered with snow. Kazan, with his three-quarters strain of dog, ran over the trail from trap to trap, intent only on something alive—meat to devour. Gray Wolf, in her blindness, scented *death*. It shivered in the tree-tops above her. She found it in every trap-house they came to—death—*man death*. It grew stronger and stronger, and she whined, and nipped Kazan's flank. And Kazan went on. Gray Wolf followed him to the edge of the clearing in which Loti's cabin stood, and then she sat back on her haunches, raised her blind face to the gray sky, and gave a long and wailing cry. In that moment the bristles began to stand up along Kazan's spine. Once, long ago, he had howled before the tepee of a master who was newly dead, and he settled back on his haunches, and gave the death-cry with Gray Wolf. He, too, scented it now. Death was in the cabin, and over the cabin there stood a sapling pole, and at the end of the pole there fluttered a strip of red cotton rag—the warning flag of the plague from Athabasca to the bay. This man, like a hundred other heroes of the North, had run up the warning before he laid himself down to die. And that same night, in the cold light of the moon, Kazan and Gray Wolf swung northward into the country of the Fond du Lac.

There preceded them a messenger from the post on Reindeer Lake, who was passing up the warning that had come from Nelson House and the country to the southeast.

"There's smallpox on the Nelson," the messenger informed Williams, at Fond du Lac, "and it has struck the Crees on Wollaston Lake. God only knows what it is doing to the Bay Indians, but we hear it is wiping out the Chippewas between the Albany and the Churchill." He left the same day with his winded dogs. "I'm off to carry word to the Reveillon people to the west," he explained.

Three days later, word came from Churchill that all of the company's servants and his majesty's subjects west of the bay should prepare themselves for the coming of the Red Terror. Williams' thin face turned as white as the paper he held, as he read the words of the Churchill factor.

"It means dig graves," he said. "That's the only preparation we can make."

He read the paper aloud to the men at Fond du Lac, and every available man was detailed to spread the warning throughout the post's territory. There was a quick harnessing of dogs, and on each sledge that went out was a roll of red cotton cloth—rolls that were ominous of death, lurid signals of pestilence and horror, whose touch sent shuddering chills through the men who were about to scatter them among the forest people. Kazan and Gray Wolf struck the trail of one of these sledges on the Gray Beaver, and followed it for half a mile. The next day, farther to the west, they struck another, and on the fourth day still a third. The last trail was fresh, and Gray Wolf drew back from it as if stung, her fangs snarling. On the wind there came to them the pungent odor of smoke. They cut at right angles to the trail, Gray Wolf leaping clear of the marks in the snow, and climbed to the cap of a ridge. To windward of them, and down in the plain, a cabin was burning. A team of huskies and a man were disappearing in the spruce forest. Deep down in his throat Kazan gave a rumbling whine. Gray Wolf stood as rigid as a rock. In the cabin a plague-dead man was burning. It was the law of the North. And the mystery of the funeral pyre came again to Kazan and Gray Wolf. This time they did not howl, but slunk down into the farther plain, and did not stop that day until they had buried themselves deep in a dry and sheltered swamp ten miles to the north.

After this they followed the days and weeks which marked the winter of nineteen hundred and ten as one of the most terrible in all the history of the Northland—a single month in which wild life as well as human hung in the balance, and when cold, starvation and plague wrote a chapter in the lives of the forest people which will not be forgotten for generations to come.

In the swamp Kazan and Gray Wolf found a home under a windfall. It was a small comfortable nest, shut in entirely from the snow and wind. Gray Wolf took possession of it immediately. She flattened herself out on her belly, and panted to show Kazan her contentment and satisfaction. Nature again kept Kazan close at her side. A vision came to him, unreal and dream-like, of that wonderful night under the stars—ages and ages ago, it seemed—when he had fought the leader of the wolf-pack, and young Gray Wolf had crept to his side after his victory and had given herself to him for mate. But this mating season there was no running after the doe or the caribou, or mingling with the wild pack. They lived chiefly on rabbit and spruce partridge, because of Gray Wolf's blindness. Kazan could hunt those alone. The hair had now grown over Gray Wolf's sightless eyes. She had ceased to grieve, to rub her eyes with her paws, to whine for the sunlight, the golden moon and the stars. Slowly she began to forget that she had ever seen those things. She could now run more swiftly at Kazan's flank. Scent and hearing had become wonderfully keen. She could wind a caribou two miles distant, and the presence of man she could pick up at an even greater distance. On a still night she had heard the splash of a trout half a mile away. And as these two things—scent and hearing—became more and more developed in her, those same senses became less active in Kazan.

He began to depend upon Gray Wolf. She would point out the hiding-place of a partridge fifty yards from their trail. In their hunts she became the leader—until game was found. And as Kazan learned to trust to her in the hunt, so he began just as instinctively to heed her warnings. If Gray Wolf reasoned, it was to the effect that without Kazan she would die. She had tried hard now and then to catch a partridge, or a rabbit, but she had always failed. Kazan meant life to her. And—if she reasoned—it was to make herself indispensable to her mate. Blindness had made her different than she would otherwise have been. Again nature promised motherhood to her. But she did not—as she would have done in the open, and with sight—hold more and more aloof from Kazan as the days passed. It was her habit, spring, summer and winter, to snuggle close to Kazan and lie with her beautiful head resting on his neck or back. If Kazan snarled at her she did not snap back, but slunk down as though struck a blow. With her warm tongue she would lick away the ice that froze to the long hair between Kazan's toes. For days after he had run a sliver in his paw she nursed his foot. Blindness had made Kazan absolutely necessary to her existence—and now, in a different way, she became more and more necessary to Kazan. They were happy in their swamp home. There was plenty of small game about them, and it was warm under the windfall. Rarely did they go beyond the limits of the swamp to hunt. Out on the more distant plains and the barren ridges they occasionally heard the cry of the wolf-pack on the trail of meat, but it no longer thrilled them with a desire to join in the chase.

One day they struck farther than usual to the west. They left the swamp, crossed a plain over which a fire had swept the preceding year, climbed a ridge, and descended into a second plain. At the bottom Gray Wolf stopped and sniffed the air. At these times Kazan always watched her, waiting eagerly and nervously if the scent was too faint for him to catch. But to-day he caught the edge of it, and he knew why Gray Wolf's ears flattened, and her hindquarters drooped. The scent of game would have made her rigid and alert. But it was not the game smell. It was human, and Gray Wolf slunk behind Kazan and whined. For several minutes they stood without moving or making a sound, and then Kazan led the way on. Less than three hundred yards away they came to a thick clump of scrub spruce, and almost ran into a snow-smothered tepee. It was abandoned. Life and fire had not been there for a long time. But from the tepee had come the man-smell. With legs rigid and his spine quivering Kazan approached the opening to the tepee. He looked in. In the middle of the tepee, lying on the charred embers of a fire, lay a ragged blanket—and in the blanket was wrapped the body of a little Indian child. Kazan could see the tiny moccasined feet. But so long had death been there that he could scarcely smell the presence of it. He drew back, and saw Gray Wolf cautiously nosing about a long and peculiarly shaped hummock in the snow. She had traveled about it three times, but never approaching nearer than a man could have reached with a rifle barrel. At the end of her third circle she sat down on her haunches, and Kazan went close to the hummock and sniffed. Under that bulge in the snow, as well as in the tepee, there was death. They slunk away, their ears flattened and their tails drooping until they trailed the snow, and did not stop until they reached their swamp home. Even there Gray Wolf still sniffed the horror of the plague, and her muscles twitched and shivered as she lay close at Kazan's side.

That night the big white moon had around its edge a crimson rim. It meant cold—intense cold. Always the plague came in the days of greatest cold—the lower the temperature the more terrible its havoc. It grew steadily colder that night, and the increased chill penetrated to the heart of the windfall, and drew Kazan and Gray Wolf closer together. With dawn, which came at about eight o'clock, Kazan and his blind mate sallied forth into the day. It was fifty degrees below zero. About them the trees cracked with reports like pistol-shots. In the thickest spruce the partridges were humped into round balls of feathers. The snow-shoe rabbits had burrowed deep under the snow or to the heart of the heaviest windfalls. Kazan and Gray Wolf found few fresh trails, and after an hour of fruitless hunting they returned to their lair. Kazan, dog-like, had buried the half of a rabbit two or three days before, and they dug this out of the snow and ate the frozen flesh.

All that day it grew colder—steadily colder. The night that followed was cloudless, with a white moon and brilliant stars. The temperature had fallen another ten degrees, and nothing was moving. Traps were never sprung on such nights, for even the furred things—the mink, and the ermine, and the lynx—lay snug in the holes and the nests they had found for themselves. An increasing hunger was not strong enough to drive Kazan and Gray Wolf from their windfall. The next day there was no break in the terrible cold, and toward noon Kazan set out on a hunt for meat, leaving Gray Wolf in the windfall. Being three-quarters dog, food was more necessary to Kazan than to his mate. Nature has fitted the wolf-breed for famine, and in ordinary temperature Gray Wolf could have lived for a fortnight without food. At sixty degrees below zero she could exist a week, perhaps ten days. Only thirty hours had passed sinee they had devoured the last of the frozen rabbit, and she was quite satisfied to remain in their snug retreat.

But Kazan was hungry. He began to hunt in the face of the wind, traveling toward the burned plain. He nosed about every windfall that he came to, and investigated the thickets. A thin shot-like snow had fallen, and in this—from the windfall to the burn—he found but a single trail, and that was the trail of an ermine. Under a windfall he caught the warm scent of a rabbit, but the rabbit was as safe from him there as were the partridges in the trees, and after an hour of futile digging and gnawing he gave up his effort to reach it. For three hours he had hunted when he returned to Gray Wolf. He was exhausted. While Gray Wolf, with the instinct of the wild, had saved her own strength and energy, Kazan had been burning up his reserve forces, and was hungrier than ever.

The moon rose clear and brilliant in the sky again that night, and Kazan set out once more on the hunt. He urged Gray Wolf to accompany him, whining for her outside the windfall—returning for her twice—but Gray Wolf laid her ears aslant and refused to move. The temperature had now fallen to sixty-five or seventy degrees below zero, and with it there came from the north an increasing wind, making the night one in which human life could not have existed for an hour. By midnight Kazan was back under the windfall. The wind grew stronger. It began to wail in mournful dirges over the swamp, and then it burst in fierce shrieking volleys, with intervals of quiet between. These were the first warnings from the great barrens that lay between the last lines of timber and the Arctic. With morning the storm burst in all its fury from out of the north, and Gray Wolf and Kazan lay close together and shivered as they listened to the roar of it over the windfall. Once Kazan thrust his head and shoulders out from the shelter of the fallen trees, but the storm drove him back. Everything that possessed life had sought shelter, according to its way and instinct. The furred creatures like the mink and the ermine were safest, for during the warmer hunting days they were of the kind that cached meat. The wolves and the foxes had sought out the windfalls, and the rocks. Winged things, with the exception of the owls, who were a tenth part body and nine-tenths feathers, burrowed under snow-drifts or found shelter in thick spruce. To the hoofed and horned animals the storm meant greatest havoc. The deer, the caribou and the moose could not crawl under windfalls or creep between rocks. The best they could do was to lie down in the lee of a drift, and allow themselves to be covered deep with the protecting snow. Even then they could not keep their shelter long, for they had to *eat*. For eighteen hours out of the twenty-four the moose had to feed to keep himself alive during the winter. His big stomach demanded quantity, and it took him most of his time to nibble from the tops of bushes the two or three bushels he needed a day. The caribou required almost as much—the deer least of the three.

And the storm kept up that day, and the next, and still a third—three days and three nights—and the third day and night there came with it a stinging, shot-like snow that fell two feet deep on the level, and in drifts of eight and ten. It was the "heavy snow" of the Indians—the snow that lay like lead on the earth, and under which partridges and rabbits were smothered in thousands.

On the fourth day after the beginning of the storm Kazan and Gray Wolf issued forth from the windfall. There was no longer a wind—no more falling snow. The whole world lay under a blanket of unbroken white, and it was intensely cold.

The plague had worked its havoc with men. Now had come the days of famine and death for the wild things.

XIII

THE TRAIL OF HUNGER

Kazan and Gray Wolf had been a hundred and forty hours without food. To Gray Wolf this meant acute discomfort, a growing weakness. To Kazan it was starvation. Six days and six nights of fasting had drawn in their ribs and put deep hollows in front of their hindquarters. Kazan's eyes were red, and they narrowed to slits as he looked forth into the day. Gray Wolf followed him this time when he went out on the hard snow. Eagerly and hopefully they began the hunt in the bitter cold. They swung around the edge of the windfall, where there had always been rabbits. There were no tracks now, and no scent. They continued in a horseshoe circle through the swamp, and the only scent they caught was that of a snow-owl perched up in a spruce. They came to the burn and turned back, hunting the opposite side of the swamp. On this side there was a ridge. They climbed the ridge, and from the cap of it looked out over a world that was barren of life. Ceaselessly Gray Wolf sniffed the air, but she gave no signal to Kazan. On the top of the ridge Kazan stood panting. His endurance was gone. On their return through the swamp he stumbled over an obstacle which he tried to clear with a jump. Hungrier and weaker, they returned to the windfall. The night that followed was clear, and brilliant with stars. They hunted the swamp again. Nothing was moving—save one other creature, and that was a fox. Instinct told them that it was futile to follow him.

It was then that the old thought of the cabin returned to Kazan. Two things the cabin had always meant to him—warmth and food. And far beyond the ridge was the cabin, where he and Gray Wolf had howled at the scent of death. He did not think of man—or of that mystery which he had howled at. He thought only of the cabin, and the cabin had always meant food. He set off in a straight line for the ridge, and Gray Wolf followed. They crossed the ridge and the burn beyond, and entered the edge of a second swamp. Kazan was hunting listlessly now. His head hung low. His bushy tail dragged in the snow. He was intent on the cabin—only the cabin. It was his last hope. But Gray Wolf was still alert, taking in the wind, and lifting her head whenever Kazan stopped to snuffle his chilled nose in the snow. At last it came—the scent! Kazan had moved on, but he stopped when he found that Gray Wolf was not following. All the strength that was in his starved body revealed itself in a sudden rigid tenseness as he looked at his mate. Her forefeet were planted firmly to the east; her slim gray head was reaching out for the scent; her body trembled.

Then—suddenly—they heard a sound, and with a whining cry Kazan set out in its direction, with Gray Wolf at his flank. The scent grew stronger and stronger in Gray Wolf's nostrils, and soon it came to Kazan. It was not the scent of a rabbit or a partridge. It was big game. They approached cautiously, keeping full in the wind. The swamp grew thicker, the spruce more dense, and now—from a hundred yards ahead of them—there came a crashing of locked and battling horns. Ten seconds more they climbed over a snowdrift, and Kazan stopped and dropped flat on his belly. Gray Wolf crouched close at his side, her blind eyes turned to what she could smell but could not see.

Fifty yards from them a number of moose had gathered for shelter in the thick spruce. They had eaten clear a space an acre in extent. The trees were cropped bare as high as they could reach, and the snow was beaten hard under their feet. There were six animals in the acre, two of them bulls—and these bulls were fighting, while three cows and a yearling were huddled in a group watching the mighty duel. Just before the storm a young bull, sleek, three-quarters grown, and with the small compact antlers of a four-year-old, had led the three cows and the yearling to this sheltered spot among the spruce. Until last night he had been master of the herd. During the night the older bull had invaded his dominion. The invader was four times as old as the young bull. He was half again as heavy. His huge palmate horns, knotted and irregular—but massive—spoke of age. A warrior of a hundred fights, he had not hesitated to give battle in his effort to rob the younger bull of his home and family. Three times they had fought since dawn, and the hard-trodden snow was red with blood. The smell of it came to Kazan's and Gray Wolf's nostrils. Kazan sniffed hungrily. Queer sounds rolled up and down in Gray Wolf's throat, and she licked her jaws.

For a moment the two fighters drew a few yards apart, and stood with lowered heads. The old bull had not yet won victory. The younger bull represented youth and endurance; in the older bull those things were pitted against craft, greater weight, maturer strength—and a head and horns that were like a battering ram. But in that great hulk of the older bull there was one other thing—age. His huge sides were panting. His nostrils were as wide as bells. Then, as if some invisible spirit of the arena had given the signal, the animals came together again. The crash of their horns could have been heard half a mile away, and under twelve hundred pounds of flesh and bone the younger hull went plunging back upon his haunches. Then was when youth displayed itself. In an instant he was up, and locking horns with his adversary. Twenty times he had done this, and each attack had seemed filled with increasing strength. And now, as if realizing that the last moments of the last fight had come, he twisted the old bull's neck and fought as he had never fought before. Kazan and Gray Wolf both heard the sharp crack that followed—as if a dry stick had been stepped upon and broken. It was February, and the hoofed animals were already beginning to shed their horns—especially the older bulls, whose palmate growths drop first. This fact gave victory to the younger bull in the blood-stained arena a few yards from Gray Wolf and Kazan. From its socket in the old bull's skull one of his huge antlers broke with that sharp snapping sound, and in another moment four inches of stiletto-like horn buried itself back of his foreleg. In an instant all hope and courage left him, and he swung backward yard by yard, with the younger bull prodding his neck and shoulders until blood dripped from him in little streams. At the edge of the clearing he flung himself free and crashed off into the forest.

The younger bull did not pursue. He tossed his head, and stood for a few moments with heaving sides and dilated nostrils, facing in the direction his vanquished foe had taken. Then he turned, and trotted back to the still motionless cows and yearling.

Kazan and Gray Wolf were quivering. Gray Wolf slunk back from the edge of the clearing, and Kazan followed. No longer were they interested in the cows and the young bull. From that clearing they had seen meat driven forth—meat that was beaten in fight, and bleeding. Every instinct of the wild pack returned to Gray Wolf now—and in Kazan the mad desire to taste the blood he smelled. Swiftly they turned toward the blood-stained trail of the old bull, and when they came to it they found it spattered red. Kazan's jaws dripped as the hot scent drove the blood like veins of fire through his weakened body. His eyes were reddened by starvation, and in them there was a light now that they had never known even in the days of the wolf-pack.

He set off swiftly, almost forgetful of Gray Wolf. But his mate no longer required his flank for guidance. With her nose close to the trail

JAMES OLIVER CURWOOD

she ran—ran as she had run in the long and thrilling hunts before blindness came. Half a mile from the spruce thicket they came upon the old bull. He had sought shelter behind a clump of balsam, and he stood over a growing pool of blood in the snow. He was still breathing hard. His massive head, grotesque now with its one antler, was drooping. Flecks of blood dropped from his distended nostrils. Even then, with the old bull weakened by starvation, exhaustion and loss of blood, a wolf-pack would have hung back before attacking. Where they would have hesitated, Kazan leaped in with a snarling cry. For an instant his fangs sunk into the thick hide of the bull's throat. Then he was flung back—twenty feet. Hunger gnawing at his vitals robbed him of all caution, and he sprang to the attack again—full at the bull's front—while Gray Wolf crept up unseen behind, seeking in her blindness the vulnerable part which nature had not taught Kazan to find.

This time Kazan was caught fairly on the broad palmate leaf of the bull's antler, and he was flung back again, half stunned. In that same moment Gray Wolf's long white teeth cut like knives through one of the bull's rope-like hamstrings. For thirty seconds she kept the hold, while the bull plunged wildly in his efforts to trample her underfoot. Kazan was quick to learn, still quicker to be guided by Gray Wolf, and he leaped in again, snapping for a hold on the bulging cord just above the knee. He missed, and as he lunged forward on his shoulders Gray Wolf was flung off. But she had accomplished her purpose. Beaten in open battle with one of his kind, and now attacked by a still deadlier foe, the old bull began to retreat. As he went, one hip sank under him at every step. The tendon of his left leg was bitten half through.

Without being able to see, Gray Wolf seemed to realize what had happened. Again she was the pack-wolf—with all the old wolf strategy. Twice flung back by the old bull's horn, Kazan knew better than to attack openly again. Gray Wolf trotted after the bull, but he remained behind for a moment to lick up hungrily mouthfuls of the blood-soaked snow. Then he followed, and ran close against Gray Wolf's side, fifty yards behind the bull. There was more blood in the trail now—a thin red ribbon of it. Fifteen minutes later the bull stopped again, and faced about, his great head lowered. His eyes were red. There was a droop to his neck and shoulders that spoke no longer of the unconquerable fighting spirit that had been a part of him for nearly a score of years. No longer was he lord of the wilderness about him; no longer was there defiance in the poise of his splendid head, or the flash of eager fire in his bloodshot eyes. His breath came with a gasping sound that was growing more and more distinct. A hunter would have known what it meant. The stiletto-point of the younger bull's antler had gone home, and the old bull's lungs were failing him. More than once Gray Wolf had heard that sound in the early days of her hunting with the pack, and she understood. Slowly she began to circle about the wounded monarch at a distance of about twenty yards. Kazan kept at her side.

Once—twice—twenty times they made that slow circle, and with each turn they made the old bull turned, and his breath grew heavier and his head drooped lower. Noon came, and was followed by the more intense cold of the last half of the day. Twenty circles became a hundred—two hundred—and more. Under Gray Wolf's and Kazan's feet the snow grew hard in the path they made. Under the old bull's widespread hoofs the snow was no longer white—but red. A thousand times before this unseen tragedy of the wilderness had been enacted. It was an epoch of that life where life itself means the survival of the fittest, where to live means to kill, and to die means to perpetuate life. At last, in that steady and deadly circling of Gray Wolf and Kazan, there came a time when the old bull did not turn—then a second, a third and a fourth time, and Gray Wolf seemed to know. With Kazan she drew back from the hard-beaten trail, and they flattened themselves on their bellies under a dwarf spruce—and waited. For many minutes the bull stood motionless, his hamstrung quarter sinking lower and lower. And then with a deep blood-choked gasp he sank down.

For a long time Kazan and Gray Wolf did not move, and when at last they returned to the beaten trail the bull's heavy head was resting on the snow. Again they began to circle, and now the circle narrowed foot by foot, until only ten yards—then nine—then eight—separated them from their prey. The bull attempted to rise, and failed. Gray Wolf heard the effort. She heard him sink back and suddenly she leaped in swiftly and silently from behind. Her sharp fangs buried themselves in the bull's nostrils, and with the first instinct of the husky, Kazan sprang for a throat hold. This time he was not flung off. It was Gray Wolf's terrible hold that gave him time to tear through the half-inch hide, and to bury his teeth deeper and deeper, until at last they reached the jugular. A gush of warm blood spurted into his face. But he did not let go. Just as he had held to the jugular of his first buck on that moonlight night a long time ago, so he held to the old bull now. It was Gray Wolf who unclamped his jaws. She drew back, sniffing the air, listening. Then, slowly, she raised her head, and through the frozen and starving wilderness there went her wailing triumphant cry—the call to meat.

For them the days of famine had passed.

XIV

The Right of Fang

After the fight Kazan lay down exhausted in the blood-stained snow, while faithful Gray Wolf, still filled with the endurance of her wild wolf breed, tore fiercely at the thick skin on the bull's neck to lay open the red flesh. When she had done this she did not eat, but ran to Kazan's side and whined softly as she muzzled him with her nose. After that they feasted, crouching side by side at the bull's neck and tearing at the warm sweet flesh.

The last pale light of the northern day was fading swiftly into night when they drew back, gorged until there were no longer hollows in their sides. The faint wind died away. The clouds that had hung in the sky during the day drifted eastward, and the moon shone brilliant and clear. For an hour the night continued to grow lighter. To the brilliance of the moon and the stars there was added now the pale fires of the aurora borealis, shivering and flashing over the Pole.

Its hissing crackling monotone, like the creaking of steel sledge-runners on frost-filled snow, came faintly to the ears of Kazan and Gray Wolf.

As yet they had not gone a hundred yards from the dead bull, and at the first sound of that strange mystery in the northern skies they stopped and listened to it, alert and suspicious. Then they laid their ears aslant and trotted slowly back to the meat they had killed. Instinct told them that it was theirs only by right of fang. They had fought to kill it. And it was in the law of the wild that they would have to fight to keep it. In good hunting days they would have gone on and wandered under the moon and the stars. But long days and nights of starvation had taught them something different now.

On that clear and stormless night following the days of plague and famine, a hundred thousand hungry creatures came out from their retreats to hunt for food. For eighteen hundred miles east and west and a thousand miles north and south, slim gaunt-bellied creatures hunted under the moon and the stars. Something told Kazan and Gray Wolf that this hunt was on, and never for an instant did they cease their vigilance. At last they lay down at the edge of the spruce thicket, and waited. Gray Wolf muzzled Kazan gently with her blind face. The uneasy whine in her throat was a warning to him. Then she sniffed the air, and listened—sniffed and listened.

Suddenly every muscle in their bodies grew rigid. Something living had passed near them, something that they could not see or hear, and scarcely scent. It came again, as mysterious as a shadow, and then out of the air there floated down as silently as a huge snowflake a great white owl. Kazan saw the hungry winged creature settle on the bull's shoulder. Like a flash he was out from his cover, Gray Wolf a yard behind him. With an angry snarl he lunged at the white robber, and his jaws snapped on empty air. His leap carried him clean over the bull. He turned, but the owl was gone.

Nearly all of his old strength had returned to him now. He trotted about the bull, the hair along his spine bristling like a brush, his eyes wide and menacing. He snarled at the still air. His jaws clicked, and he sat back on his haunches and faced the blood-stained trail that the moose had left before he died. Again that instinct as infallible as reason told him that danger would come from there.

Like a red ribbon the trail ran back through the wilderness. The little swift-moving ermine were everywhere this night, looking like white rats as they dodged about in the moonlight. They were first to find the trail, and with all the ferocity of their blood-eating nature followed it with quick exciting leaps. A fox caught the scent of it a quarter of a mile to windward, and came nearer. From out of a deep windfall a beady-eyed, thin-bellied fisher-cat came forth, and stopped with his feet in the crimson ribbon.

It was the fisher-cat that brought Kazan out; from under his cover of spruce again. In the moonlight there was a sharp quick fight, a snarling and scratching, a cat-like yowl of pain, and the fisher forgot his hunger in flight. Kazan returned to Gray Wolf with a lacerated and bleeding nose. Gray Wolf licked it sympathetically, while Kazan stood rigid and listening.

The fox swung swiftly away with the wind, warned by the sounds of conflict. He was not a fighter, but a murderer who killed from behind, and a little later he leaped upon an owl and tore it into bits for the half-pound of flesh within the mass of feathers.

But nothing could drive back those little white outlaws of the wilderness—the ermine. They would have stolen between the feet of man to get at the warm flesh and blood of the freshly killed bull. Kazan hunted them savagely. They were too quick for him, more like elusive flashes in the moonlight than things of life. They burrowed under the old bull's body and fed while he raved and filled his mouth with snow. Gray Wolf sat placidly on her haunches. The little ermine did not trouble her, and after a time Kazan realized this, and flung himself down beside her, panting and exhausted.

For a long time after that the night was almost unbroken by sound. Once in the far distance there came the cry of a wolf, and now and then, to punctuate the deathly silence, the snow owl hooted in blood-curdling protest from his home in the spruce-tops. The moon was straight above the old bull when Gray Wolf scented the first real danger. Instantly she gave the warning to Kazan and faced the bloody trail, her lithe body quivering, her fangs gleaming in the starlight, a snarling whine in her throat. Only in the face of their deadliest enemy, the lynx—the terrible fighter who had blinded her long ago in that battle on the Sun Rock!— did she give such warning as this to Kazan. He sprang ahead of her, ready for battle even before he caught the scent of the gray beautiful creature of death stealing over the trail.

Then came the interruption. From a mile away there burst forth a single fierce long-drawn howl.

After all, that was the cry of the true master of the wilderness—the wolf. It was the cry of hunger. It was the cry that sent men's blood running more swiftly through their veins, that brought the moose and the deer to their feet shivering in every limb—the cry that wailed like a note of death through swamp and forest and over the snow-smothered ridges until its faintest echoes reached for miles into the starlit night.

There was silence, and in that awesome stillness Kazan and Gray Wolf stood shoulder to shoulder facing the cry, and in response to that cry there worked within them a strange and mystic change, for what they had heard was not a warning or a menace but the call of Brotherhood. Away off there—beyond the lynx and the fox and the fisher-cat, were the creatures of their kind, the wild-wolf pack, to which the right to all flesh and blood was common—in which existed that savage socialism of the wilderness, the Brotherhood of the Wolf. And Gray Wolf, setting back on her haunches, sent forth the response to that cry—a wailing triumphant note that told her hungry brethren there was feasting at the end of the trail.

And the lynx, between those two cries, sneaked off into the wide and moonlit spaces of the forest.

XV

A Fight Under the Stars

On their haunches Kazan and Gray Wolf waited. Five minutes passed, ten—fifteen—and Gray Wolf became uneasy. No response had followed her call. Again she howled, with Kazan quivering and listening beside her, and again there followed that dead stillness of the night. This was not the way of the pack. She knew that it had not gone beyond the reach of her voice and its silence puzzled her. And then in a flash it came to them both that the pack, or the single wolf whose cry they had heard, was very near them. The scent was warm. A few moments later Kazan saw a moving object in the moonlight. It was followed by another, and still another, until there were five slouching in a half-circle about them, seventy yards away. Then they laid themselves flat in the snow and were motionless.

A snarl turned Kazan's eyes to Gray Wolf. His blind mate had drawn back. Her white fangs gleamed menacingly in the starlight. Her ears were flat. Kazan was puzzled. Why was she signaling danger to him when it was the wolf, and not the lynx, out there in the snow? And why did the wolves not come in and feast? Slowly he moved toward them, and Gray Wolf called to him with her whine. He paid no attention to her, but went on, stepping lightly, his head high in the air, his spine bristling.

In the scent of the strangers, Kazan was catching something now that was strangely familiar. It drew him toward them more swiftly and when at last he stopped twenty yards from where the little group lay flattened in the snow, his thick brush waved slightly. One of the animals sprang up and approached. The others followed and in another moment Kazan was in the midst of them, smelling and smelled, and wagging his tail. They were dogs, and not wolves.

In some lonely cabin in the wilderness their master had died, and they had taken to the forests. They still bore signs of the sledge-traces. About their necks were moose-hide collars. The hair was worn short at their flanks, and one still dragged after him three feet of corded babiche trace. Their eyes gleamed red and hungry in the glow of the moon and the stars. They were thin, and gaunt and starved, and Kazan suddenly turned and trotted ahead of them to the side of the dead bull. Then he fell back and sat proudly on his haunches beside Gray Wolf, listening to the snapping of jaws and the rending of flesh as the starved pack feasted.

Gray Wolf slunk closer to Kazan. She muzzled his neck and Kazan gave her a swift dog-like caress of his tongue, assuring her that all was well. She flattened herself in the snow when the dogs had finished and came up in their dog way to sniff at her, and make closer acquaintance with Kazan. Kazan towered over her, guarding her. One huge red-eyed dog who still dragged the bit of babiche trace muzzled Gray Wolf's soft neck for a fraction of a second too long, and Kazan uttered a savage snarl of warning. The dog drew back, and for a moment their fangs gleamed over Gray Wolf's blind face. It was the Challenge of the Breed.

The big husky was the leader of the pack, and if one of the other dogs had snarled at him, as Kazan snarled he would have leaped at his throat. But in Kazan, standing fierce and half wild over Gray Wolf, he recognized none of the serfdom of the sledge-dogs. It was master facing master; in Kazan it was more than that for he was Gray Wolf's mate. In an instant more he would have leaped over her body to have fought for her, more than for the right of leadership. But the big husky turned away sullenly, growling, still snarling, and vented his rage by nipping fiercely at the flank of one of his sledge-mates.

Gray Wolf understood what had happened, though she could not see. She shrank closer to Kazan. She knew that the moon and the stars had looked down on that thing that always meant death—the challenge to the right of mate. With her luring coyness, whining and softly muzzling his shoulder and neck, she tried to draw Kazan away from the pad-beaten circle in which the bull lay. Kazan's answer was an ominous rolling of smothered thunder deep down in his throat. He lay down beside her, licked her blind face swiftly, and faced the stranger dogs.

The moon sank lower and lower and at last dropped behind the western forests. The stars grew paler. One by one they faded from the sky and after a time there followed the cold gray dawn of the North. In that dawn the big husky leader rose from the hole he had made in the snow and returned to the bull. Kazan, alert, was on his feet in an instant and stood also close to the bull. The two circled ominously, their heads lowered, their crests bristling. The husky drew away, and Kazan crouched at the bull's neck and began tearing at the frozen flesh. He

JAMES OLIVER CURWOOD

was not hungry. But in this way he showed his right to the flesh, his defiance of the right of the big husky.

For a few seconds he forgot Gray Wolf. The husky had slipped back like a shadow and now he stood again over Gray Wolf, sniffing her neck and body. Then he whined. In that whine were the passion, the invitation, the demand of the Wild. So quickly that the eye could scarcely follow her movement faithful Gray Wolf sank her gleaming fangs in the husky's shoulder.

A gray streak—nothing more tangible than a streak of gray, silent and terrible, shot through the dawn-gloom. It was Kazan. He came without a snarl, without a cry, and in a moment he and the husky were in the throes of terrific battle.

The four other huskies ran in quickly and stood waiting a dozen paces from the combatants. Gray Wolf lay crouched on her belly. The giant husky and the quarter-strain wolf-dog were not fighting like sledge-dog or wolf. For a few moments rage and hatred made them fight like mongrels. Both had holds. Now one was down, and now the other, and so swiftly did they change their positions that the four waiting sledge-dogs were puzzled and stood motionless. Under other conditions they would have leaped upon the first of the fighters to be thrown upon his back and torn him to pieces. That was the way of the wolf and the wolf-dog. But now they stood back, hesitating and fearful.

The big husky had never been beaten in battle. Great Dane ancestors had given him a huge bulk and a jaw that could crush an ordinary dog's head. But in Kazan he was meeting not only the dog and the wolf, but all that was best in the two. And Kazan had the advantage of a few hours of rest and a full stomach. More than that, he was fighting for Gray Wolf. His fangs had sunk deep in the husky's shoulder, and the husky's long teeth met through the hide and flesh of his neck. An inch deeper, and they would have pierced his jugular. Kazan knew this, as he crunched his enemy's shoulder-bone, and every instant—even in their fiercest struggling—he was guarding against a second and more successful lunge of those powerful jaws.

At last the lunge came, and quicker than the wolf itself Kazan freed himself and leaped back. His chest dripped blood, but he did not feel the hurt. They began slowly to circle, and now the watching sledge-dogs drew a step or two nearer, and their jaws drooled nervously and their red eyes glared as they waited for the fatal moment. Their eyes were on the big husky. He became the pivot of Kazan's wider circle now, and he limped as he turned. His shoulder was broken. His ears were flattened as he watched Kazan.

Kazan's ears were erect, and his feet touched the snow lightly. All his fighting cleverness and all his caution had returned to him. The blind rage of a few moments was gone and he fought now as he had fought his deadliest enemy, the long-clawed lynx. Five times he circled around the husky, and then like a shot he was in, sending his whole weight against the husky's shoulder, with the momentum of a ten-foot leap behind it. This time he did not try for a hold, but slashed at the husky's jaws. It was the deadliest of all attacks when that merciless tribunal of death stood waiting for the first fall of the vanquished. The huge dog was thrown from his feet. For a fatal moment he rolled upon his side and in the moment his four sledge-mates were upon him. All of their hatred of the weeks and months in which the long-fanged leader had bullied them in the traces was concentrated upon him now and he was literally torn into pieces.

Kazan pranced to Gray Wolf's side and with a joyful whine she laid her head over his neck. Twice he had fought the Fight of Death for her. Twice he had won. And in her blindness Gray Wolf's soul—if soul she had—rose in exultation to the cold gray sky, and her breast panted against Kazan's shoulder as she listened to the crunching of fangs in the flesh and bone of the foe her lord and master had overthrown.

XVI

THE CALL

Followed days of feasting on the frozen flesh of the old bull. In vain Gray Wolf tried to lure Kazan off into the forests and the swamps. Day by day the temperature rose. There was hunting now. And Gray Wolf wanted to be alone—with Kazan. But with Kazan, as with most men, leadership and power roused new sensations. And he was the leader of the dog-pack, as he had once been a leader among the wolves. Not only Gray Wolf followed at his flank now, but the four huskies trailed behind him. Once more he was experiencing that triumph and strange thrill that he had almost forgotten and only Gray Wolf, in that eternal night of her blindness, felt with dread foreboding the danger into which his newly achieved czarship might lead him.

For three days and three nights they remained in the neighborhood of the dead moose, ready to defend it against others, and yet each day and each night growing less vigilant in their guard. Then came the fourth night, on which they killed a young doe. Kazan led in that chase and for the first time, in the excitement of having the pack at his back, he left his blind mate behind. When they came to the kill he was the first to leap at its soft throat. And not until he had begun to tear at the doe's flesh did the others dare to eat. He was master. He could send them back with a snarl. At the gleam of his fangs they crouched quivering on their bellies in the snow.

Kazan's blood was fomented with brute exultation, and the excitement and fascination that came in the possession of new power took the place of Gray Wolf each day a little more. She came in half an hour after the kill, and there was no longer the lithesome alertness to her slender legs, or gladness in the tilt of her ears or the poise of her head. She did not eat much of the doe. Her blind face was turned always in Kazan's direction. Wherever he moved she followed with her unseeing eyes, as if expecting each moment his old signal to her—that low throat-note that had called to her so often when they were alone in the wilderness.

In Kazan, as leader of the pack, there was working a curious change. If his mates had been wolves it would not have been difficult for Gray

Wolf to have lured him away. But Kazan was among his own kind. He was a dog. And they were dogs. Fires that had burned down and ceased to warm him flamed up in him anew. In his life with Gray Wolf one thing had oppressed him as it could not oppress her, and that thing was loneliness. Nature had created him of that kind which requires companionship—not of one but of many. It had given him birth that he might listen to and obey the commands of the voice of man. He had grown to hate men, but of the dogs—his kind—he was a part. He had been happy with Gray Wolf, happier than he had ever been in the companionship of men and his blood-brothers. But he had been a long time separated from the life that had once been his and the call of blood made him for a time forget. And only Gray Wolf, with that wonderful super-instinct which nature was giving her in place of her lost sight, foresaw the end to which it was leading him.

Each day the temperature continued to rise until when the sun was warmest the snow began to thaw a little. This was two weeks after the fight near the bull. Gradually the pack had swung eastward, until it was now fifty miles east and twenty miles south of the old home under the windfall. More than ever Gray Wolf began to long for their old nest under the fallen trees. Again with those first promises of spring in sunshine and air, there was coming also for the second time in her life the promise of approaching motherhood.

But her efforts to draw Kazan back were unavailing, and in spite of her protest he wandered each day a little farther east and south at the head of his pack.

Instinct impelled the four huskies to move in that direction. They had not yet been long enough a part of the wild to forget the necessity of man and in that direction there was man. In that direction, and not far from them now, was the Hudson Bay Company's post to which they and their dead master owed their allegiance. Kazan did not know this, but one day something happened to bring back visions and desires that widened still more the gulf between him and Gray Wolf.

They had come to the cap of a ridge when something stopped them. It was a man's voice crying shrilly that word of long ago that had so often stirred the blood in Kazan's own veins—*"m'hoosh! m'hoosh! m'hoosh!"*— and from the ridge they looked down upon the open space of the plain, where a team of six dogs was trotting ahead of a sledge, with a man running behind them, urging them on at every other step with that cry of *"m'hoosh! m'hoosh! m'hoosh!"*

JAMES OLIVER CURWOOD

Trembling and undecided, the four huskies and the wolf-dog stood on the ridge with Gray Wolf cringing behind them. Not until man and dogs and sledge had disappeared did they move, and then they trotted down to the trail and sniffed at it whiningly and excitedly. For a mile or two they followed it, Kazan and his mates going fearlessly in the trail. Gray Wolf hung back, traveling twenty yards to the right of them, with the hot man-scent driving the blood feverishly through her brain. Only her love for Kazan—and the faith she still had in him—kept her that near.

At the edge of a swamp Kazan halted and turned away from the trail. With the desire that was growing in him there was still that old suspicion which nothing could quite wipe out—the suspicion that was an inheritance of his quarter-strain of wolf. Gray Wolf whined joyfully when he turned into the forest, and drew so close to him that her shoulder rubbed against Kazan's as they traveled side by side.

The "slush" snows followed fast after this. And the "slush" snows meant spring—and the emptying of the wilderness of human life. Kazan and his mates soon began to scent the presence and the movement of this life. They were now within thirty miles of the post. For a hundred miles on all sides of them the trappers were moving in with their late winter's catch of furs. From east and west, south and north, all trails led to the post. The pack was caught in the mesh of them. For a week not a day passed that they did not cross a fresh trail, and sometimes two or three.

Gray Wolf was haunted by constant fear. In her blindness she knew that they were surrounded by the menace of men. To Kazan what was coming to pass had more and more ceased to fill him with fear and caution. Three times that week he heard the shouts of men—and once he heard a white man's laughter and the barking of dogs as their master tossed them their daily feed of fish. In the air he caught the pungent scent of camp-fires and one night, in the far distance, he heard a wild snatch of song, followed by the yelping and barking of a dog-pack.

Slowly and surely the lure of man drew him nearer to the post—a mile to-night, two miles to-morrow, but always nearer. And Gray Wolf, fighting her losing fight to the end, sensed in the danger-filled air the nearness of that hour when he would respond to the final call and she would be left alone.

These were days of activity and excitement at the fur company's post, the days of accounting, of profit and of pleasure;—the days when the wilderness poured in its treasure of fur, to be sent a little later to London and Paris and the capitals of Europe. And this year there was more than the usual interest in the foregathering of the forest people. The plague had wrought its terrible havoc, and not until the fur-hunters had come to answer to the spring roll-call would it be known accurately who had lived and who had died.

The Chippewans and half-breeds from the south began to arrive first, with their teams of mongrel curs, picked up along the borders of civilization. Close after them came the hunters from the western barren lands, bringing with them loads of white fox and caribou skins, and an army of big-footed, long-legged Mackenzie hounds that pulled like horses and wailed like whipped puppies when the huskies and Eskimo dogs set upon them. Packs of fierce Labrador dogs, never vanquished except by death, came from close to Hudson's Bay. Team after team of little yellow and gray Eskimo dogs, as quick with their fangs as were their black and swift-running masters with their hands and feet, met the much larger and dark-colored Malemutes from the Athabasca. Enemies of all these packs of fierce huskies trailed in from all sides, fighting, snapping and snarling, with the lust of killing deep born in them from their wolf progenitors.

There was no cessation in the battle of the fangs. It began with the first brute arrivals. It continued from dawn through the day and around the camp-fires at night. There was never an end to the strife between the dogs, and between the men and the dogs. The snow was trailed and stained with blood and the scent of it added greater fierceness to the wolf-breeds.

Half a dozen battles were fought to the death each day and night. Those that died were chiefly the south-bred curs—mixtures of mastiff, Great Dane, and sheep-dog—and the fatally slow Mackenzie hounds. About the post rose the smoke of a hundred camp-fires, and about these fires gathered the women and the children of the hunters. When the snow was no longer fit for sledging, Williams, the factor, noted that there were many who had not come, and the accounts of these he later scratched out of his ledgers knowing that they were victims of the plague.

At last came the night of the Big Carnival, For weeks and months women and children and men had been looking forward to this. In scores of forest cabins, in smoke-blackened tepees, and even in the frozen homes of the little Eskimos, anticipation of this wild night of

JAMES OLIVER CURWOOD

pleasure had given an added zest to life. It was the Big Circus—the good time given twice each year by the company to its people.

This year, to offset the memory of plague and death, the factor had put forth unusual exertions. His hunters had killed four fat caribou. In the clearing there were great piles of dry logs, and in the center of all there rose eight ten-foot tree-butts crotched at the top; and from crotch to crotch there rested a stout sapling stripped of bark, and on each sapling was spitted the carcass of a caribou, to be roasted whole by the heat of the fire beneath. The fires were lighted at dusk, and Williams himself started the first of those wild songs of the Northland—the song of the caribou, as the flames leaped up into the dark night.

> *"Oh, ze cariboo-oo-oo, ze cariboo-oo-oo,*
> *He roas' on high,*
> *Jes' under ze sky.*
> *air-holes beeg white cariboo-oo-oo!"*

"Now!" he yelled. "Now—all together!" And carried away by his enthusiasm, the forest people awakened from their silence of months, and the song burst forth in a savage frenzy that reached to the skies.

Two MILES TO THE SOUTH and west that first thunder of human voice reached the ears of Kazan and Gray Wolf and the masterless huskies. And with the voices of men they heard now the excited howlings of dogs. The huskies faced the direction of the sounds, moving restlessly and whining. For a few moments Kazan stood as though carven of rock. Then he turned his head, and his first look was to Gray Wolf. She had slunk back a dozen feet and lay crouched under the thick cover of a balsam shrub. Her body, legs and neck were flattened in the snow. She made no sound, but her lips were drawn back and her teeth shone white.

Kazan trotted back to her, sniffed at her blind face and whined. Gray Wolf still did not move. He returned to the dogs and his jaws opened and closed with a snap. Still more clearly came the wild voice of the carnival, and no longer to be held back by Kazan's leadership, the four huskies dropped their heads and slunk like shadows in its direction. Kazan hesitated, urging Gray Wolf. But not a muscle of Gray Wolf's body moved. She would have followed him in face of fire but not in face of man. Not a sound escaped her ears. She heard the quick fall of Kazan's feet as he left her. In another moment she knew that he was gone. Then—and not until then—did she lift her head, and from her soft throat there broke a whimpering cry.

It was her last call to Kazan. But stronger than that there was running through Kazan's excited blood the call of man and of dog. The huskies were far in advance of him now and for a few moments he raced madly to overtake them. Then he slowed down until he was trotting, and a hundred yards farther on he stopped. Less than a mile away he could see where the flames of the great fires were reddening the sky. He gazed back to see if Gray Wolf was following and then went on until he struck an open and hard traveled trail. It was beaten with the footprints of men and dogs, and over it two of the caribou had been dragged a day or two before.

At last he came to the thinned out strip of timber that surrounded the clearing and the flare of the flames was in his eyes. The bedlam of sound that came to him now was like fire in his brain. He heard the song and the laughter of men, the shrill cries of women and children, the barking and snarling and fighting of a hundred dogs. He wanted to rush out and join them, to become again a part of what he had once been. Yard by yard he sneaked through the thin timber until he reached the edge of the clearing. There he stood in the shadow of a spruce and looked out upon life as he had once lived it, trembling, wistful and yet hesitating in that final moment.

A hundred yards away was the savage circle of men and dogs and fire. His nostrils were filled with the rich aroma of the roasting caribou, and as he crouched down, still with that wolfish caution that Gray Wolf had taught him, men with long poles brought the huge carcasses crashing down upon the melting snow about the fires. In one great rush the horde of wild revelers crowded in with bared knives, and a snarling mass of dogs closed in behind them. In another moment he had forgotten Gray Wolf, had forgotten all that man and the wild had taught him, and like a gray streak was across the open.

The dogs were surging back when he reached them, with half a dozen of the factor's men lashing them in the faces with long caribou-gut whips. The sting of a lash fell in a fierce cut over an Eskimo dog's shoulder, and in snapping at the lash his fangs struck Kazan's rump. With lightning swiftness Kazan returned the cut, and in an instant the jaws of the dogs had met. In another instant they were down and Kazan had the Eskimo dog by the throat.

With shouts the men rushed in. Again and again their whips cut like knives through the air. Their blows fell on Kazan, who was uppermost, and as he felt the burning pain of the scourging whips there flooded through him all at once the fierce memory of the days of old—the days of the Club and the Lash. He snarled. Slowly he loosened his hold of the Eskimo dog's throat. And then, out of the mêlée of dogs and men, there sprang another man—*with a club*! It fell on Kazan's back and the force of it sent him flat into the snow. It was raised again. Behind the club there was a face—a brutal, fire-reddened face. It was such a face that had driven Kazan into the wild, and as the club fell again he evaded the full weight of its blow and his fangs gleamed like ivory knives. A third time the club was raised, and this time Kazan met it in mid-air, and his teeth ripped the length of the man's forearm.

"Good God!" shrieked the man in pain, and Kazan caught the gleam of a rifle barrel as he sped toward the forest. A shot followed. Something like a red-hot coal ran the length of Kazan's hip, and deep in the forest he stopped to lick at the burning furrow where the bullet had gone just deep enough to take the skin and hair from his flesh.

GRAY WOLF WAS STILL WAITING under the balsam shrub when Kazan returned to her. Joyously she sprang forth to meet him. Once more the man had sent back the old Kazan to her. He muzzled her neck and face, and stood for a few moments with his head resting across her back, listening to the distant sound.

Then, with ears laid flat, he set out straight into the north and west. And now Gray Wolf ran shoulder to shoulder with him like the Gray Wolf of the days before the dog-pack came; for that wonderful thing that lay beyond the realm of reason told her that once more she was comrade and mate, and that their trail that night was leading to their old home under the windfall.

XVII

His Son

It happened that Kazan was to remember three things above all others. He could never quite forget his old days in the traces, though they were growing more shadowy and indistinct in his memory as the summers and the winters passed. Like a dream there came to him a memory of the time he had gone down to Civilization. Like dreams were the visions that rose before him now and then of the face of the First Woman, and of the faces of masters who—to him—had lived ages ago. And never would he quite forget the Fire, and his fights with man and beast, and his long chases in the moonlight. But two things were always with him as if they had been but yesterday, rising clear and unforgetable above all others, like the two stars in the North that never lost their brilliance. One was Woman. The other was the terrible fight of that night on the top of the Sun Rock, when the lynx had blinded forever his wild mate, Gray Wolf. Certain events remain indelibly fixed in the minds of men; and so, in a not very different way, they remain in the minds of beasts. It takes neither brain nor reason to measure the depths of sorrow or of happiness. And Kazan in his unreasoning way knew that contentment and peace, a full stomach, and caresses and kind words instead of blows had come to him through Woman, and that comradeship in the wilderness—faith, loyalty and devotion—were a part of Gray Wolf. The third unforgetable thing was about to occur in the home they had found for themselves under the swamp windfall during the days of cold and famine.

They had left the swamp over a month before when it was smothered deep in snow. On the day they returned to it the sun was shining warmly in the first glorious days of spring warmth. Everywhere, big and small, there were the rushing torrents of melting snows and the crackle of crumbling ice, the dying cries of thawing rock and earth and tree, and each night for many nights past the cold pale glow of the aurora borealis had crept farther and farther toward the Pole in fading glory. So early as this the poplar buds had begun to swell and the air was filled with the sweet odor of balsam, spruce and cedar. Where there had been famine and death and stillness six weeks before, Kazan and

Gray Wolf now stood at the edge of the swamp and breathed the earthy smells of spring, and listened to the sounds of life. Over their heads a pair of newly-mated moose-birds fluttered and scolded at them. A big jay sat pluming himself in the sunshine. Farther in they heard the crack of a stick broken under a heavy hoof. From the ridge behind them they caught the raw scent of a mother bear, busy pulling down the tender poplar buds for her six-weeks-old cubs, born while she was still deep in her winter sleep.

In the warmth of the sun and the sweetness of the air there breathed to Gray Wolf the mystery of matehood and of motherhood. She whined softly and rubbed her blind face against Kazan. For days, in her way, she tried to tell him. More than ever she wanted to curl herself up in that warm dry nest under the windfall. She had no desire to hunt. The crack of the dry stick under a cloven hoof and the warm scent of the she-bear and her cubs roused none of the old instincts in her. She wanted to curl herself up in the old windfall—and wait. And she tried hard to make Kazan understand her desire.

Now that the snow was gone they found that a narrow creek lay between them and the knoll on which the windfall was situated. Gray Wolf picked up her ears at the tumult of the little torrent. Since the day of the Fire, when Kazan and she had saved themselves on the sand-bar, she had ceased to have the inherent wolf horror of water. She followed fearlessly, even eagerly, behind Kazan as he sought a place where they could ford the rushing little stream. On the other side Kazan could see the big windfall. Gray Wolf could *smell* it and she whined joyously, with her blind face turned toward it. A hundred yards up the stream a big cedar had fallen over it and Kazan began to cross. For a moment Gray Wolf hesitated, and then followed. Side by side they trotted to the windfall. With their heads and shoulders in the dark opening to their nest they scented the air long and cautiously. Then they entered. Kazan heard Gray Wolf as she flung herself down on the dry floor of the snug cavern. She was panting, not from exhaustion, but because she was filled with a sensation of contentment and happiness. In the darkness Kazan's own jaws fell apart. He, too, was glad to get back to their old home. He went to Gray Wolf and, panting still harder, she licked his face. It had but one meaning. And Kazan understood.

For a moment he lay down beside her, listening, and eyeing the opening to their nest. Then he began to sniff about the log walls. He was close to the opening when a sudden fresh scent came to him, and he grew rigid, and his bristles stood up. The scent was followed by a whimpering, babyish chatter. A porcupine entered the opening and proceeded to advance in its foolish fashion, still chattering in that babyish way that has made its life inviolable at the hands of man. Kazan had heard that sound before, and like all other beasts had learned to ignore the presence of the innocuous creature that made it. But just now he did not stop to consider that what he saw was a porcupine and that at his first snarl the good-humored little creature would waddle away as fast as it could, still chattering baby talk to itself. His first reasoning was that it was a live thing invading the home to which Gray Wolf and he had just returned. A day later, or perhaps an hour later, he would have driven it back with a growl. Now he leaped upon it.

A wild chattering, intermingled with pig-like squeaks, and then a rising staccato of howls followed the attack. Gray Wolf sprang to the opening. The porcupine was rolled up in a thousand-spiked ball a dozen feet away, and she could hear Kazan tearing about in the throes of the direst agony that can befall a beast of the forests. His face and nose were a mat of quills. For a few moments he rolled and dug in the wet mold and earth, pawing madly at the things that pierced his flesh. Then he set off like all dogs will who have come into contact with the friendly porcupine, and raced again and again around the windfall, howling at every jump. Gray Wolf took the matter coolly. It is possible that at times there are moments of humor in the lives of animals. If so, she saw this one. She scented the porcupine and she knew that Kazan was full of quills. As there was nothing to do and nothing to fight she sat back on her haunches and waited, pricking up her ears every time Kazan passed her in his mad circuit around the windfall. At his fourth or fifth heat the porcupine smoothed itself down a little, and continuing the interrupted thread of its chatter waddled to a near-by poplar, climbed it and began to gnaw the tender bark from a limb.

At last Kazan halted before Gray Wolf. The first agony of a hundred little needles piercing his flesh had deadened into a steady burning pain. Gray Wolf went over to him and investigated him cautiously. With her teeth she seized the ends of two or three of the quills and pulled them out. Kazan was very much dog now. He gave a yelp, and whimpered as Gray Wolf jerked out a second bunch of quills. Then he flattened himself on his belly, stretched out his forelegs, closed his eyes, and without any other sound except an occasional yelp of pain allowed Gray Wolf to go on with the operation. Fortunately he had escaped getting any of the quills in his mouth and tongue. But his nose and jaws were soon red with blood. For an hour Gray Wolf kept faithfully at her task and by the end of that time had succeeded in pulling out most of the quills. A few still remained, too short and too deeply inbedded for her to extract with her teeth.

After this Kazan went down to the creek and buried his burning muzzle in the cold water. This gave him some relief, but only for a short time. The quills that remained worked their way deeper and deeper into his flesh, like living things. Nose and lips began to swell. Blood and saliva dripped from his mouth and his eyes grew red. Two hours after Gray Wolf had retired to her nest under the windfall a quill had completely pierced his lip and began to prick his tongue. In desperation Kazan chewed viciously upon a piece of wood. This broke and crumpled the quill, and destroyed its power to do further harm. Nature had told him the one thing to do to save himself. Most of that day he spent in gnawing at wood and crunching mouthfuls of earth and mold between his jaws. In this way the barb-toothed points of the quills were dulled and broken as they came through. At dusk he crawled under the windfall, and Gray Wolf gently licked his muzzle with her soft cool tongue. Frequently during the night Kazan went to the creek and found relief in its ice-cold water.

The next day he had what the forest people call "porcupine mumps." His face was swollen until Gray Wolf would have laughed if she had been human, and not blind. His chops bulged like cushions. His eyes were mere slits. When he went out into the day he blinked, for he could see scarcely better than his sightless mate. But the pain was mostly gone. The night that followed he began to think of hunting, and the next morning before it was yet dawn he brought a rabbit into their den. A few hours later he would have brought a spruce partridge to Gray Wolf, but just as he was about to spring upon his feathered prey the soft chatter of a porcupine a few yards away brought him to a sudden stop. Few things could make Kazan drop his tail. But that inane and incoherent prattle of the little spiked beast sent him off at double-quick with his tail between his legs. As man abhors and evades the creeping serpent, so Kazan would hereafter evade this little creature of the forests that never in animal history has been known to lose its good-humor or pick a quarrel.

Two weeks of lengthening days, of increasing warmth, of sunshine and hunting, followed Kazan's adventure with the porcupine. The last of the snow went rapidly. Out of the earth began to spring tips of green. The *bakneesh* vine glistened redder each day, the poplar buds began to split, and in the sunniest spots, between the rocks of the ridges the little white snow-flowers began to give a final proof that spring had come. For the first of those two weeks Gray Wolf hunted frequently with Kazan. They did not go far. The swamp was alive with small game and each day or night they killed fresh meat. After the first week Gray Wolf hunted less. Then came the soft and balmy night, glorious in the radiance of a full spring moon when she refused to leave the windfall. Kazan did not urge her. Instinct made him understand, and he did not go far from the windfall that night in his hunt. When he returned he brought a rabbit.

Came then the night when from the darkest corner of the windfall Gray Wolf warned him back with a low snarl. He stood in the opening, a rabbit between his jaws. He took no offense at the snarl, but stood for a moment, gazing into the gloom where Gray Wolf had hidden herself. Then he dropped the rabbit and lay down squarely in the opening. After a little he rose restlessly and went outside. But he did not leave the windfall. It was day when he reentered. He sniffed, as he had sniffed once before a long time ago, between the boulders at the top of the Sun Rock. That which was in the air was no longer a mystery to him. He came nearer and Gray Wolf did not snarl. She whined coaxingly as he touched her. Then his muzzle found something else. It was soft and warm and made a queer little sniffling sound. There was a responsive whine in his throat, and in the darkness came the quick soft caress of Gray Wolf's tongue. Kazan returned to the sunshine and stretched himself out before the door of the windfall. His jaws dropped open, for he was filled with a strange contentment.

XVIII

THE EDUCATION OF BA-REE

Robbed once of the joys of parenthood by the murder on the Sun Rock, both Gray Wolf and Kazan were different from what they would have been had the big gray lynx not come into their lives at that time. As if it were but yesterday they remembered the moonlit night when the lynx brought blindness to Gray Wolf and destroyed her young, and when Kazan had avenged himself and his mate in his terrible fight to the death with their enemy. And now, with that soft little handful of life snuggling close up against her, Gray Wolf saw through her blind eyes the tragic picture of that night more vividly than ever and she quivered at every sound, ready to leap in the face of an unseen foe, to rend all flesh that was not the flesh of Kazan. And ceaselessly, the slightest sound bringing him to his feet, Kazan watched and guarded. He mistrusted the moving shadows. The snapping of a twig drew back his upper lip. His fangs gleamed menacingly when the soft air brought a strange scent. In him, too, the memory of the Sun Rock, the death of their first young and the blinding of Gray Wolf, had given birth to a new instinct. Not for an instant was he off his guard. As surely as one expects the sun to rise so did he expect that sooner or later their deadly enemy would creep on them from out of the forest. In another hour such as this the lynx had brought death. The lynx had brought blindness. And so day and night he waited and watched for the lynx to come again. And woe unto any other creature of flesh and blood that dared approach the windfall in these first days of Gray Wolf's motherhood!

But peace had spread its wings of sunshine and plenty over the swamp. There were no intruders, unless the noisy whisky-jacks, the big-eyed moose-birds, the chattering bush sparrows, and the wood-mice and ermine could be called such. After the first day or two Kazan went more frequently into the windfall, and though more than once he nosed searchingly about Gray Wolf he could find only the one little pup. A little farther west the Dog-Ribs would have called the pup Ba-ree for two reasons—because he had no brothers or sisters, and because he was a mixture of dog and wolf. He was a sleek and lively little fellow from the beginning, for there was no division of mother strength and attention. He developed with the true swiftness of the wolf-whelp, and not with the slowness of the dog-pup.

For three days he was satisfied to cuddle close against his mother, feeding when he was hungry, sleeping a great deal and preened and laundered almost constantly by Gray Wolf's affectionate tongue. From the fourth day he grew busier and more inquisitive with every hour. He found his mother's blind face, with tremendous effort he tumbled over her paws, and once he lost himself completely and sniffled for help when he rolled fifteen or eighteen inches away from her. It was not long after this that he began to recognize Kazan as a part of his mother, and he was scarcely more than a week old when he rolled himself up contentedly between Kazan's forelegs and went to sleep. Kazan was puzzled. Then with a deep sigh Gray Wolf laid her head across one of her mate's forelegs, with her nose touching her runaway baby, and seemed vastly contented. For half an hour Kazan did not move.

When he was ten days old Ba-ree discovered there was great sport in tussling with a bit of rabbit fur. It was a little later when he made his second exciting discovery—light and sunshine. The sun had now reached a point where in the middle of the afternoon a bright gleam of it found its way through an overhead opening in the windfall. At first Ba-ree would only stare at the golden streak. Then came the time when he tried to play with it as he played with the rabbit fur. Each day thereafter he went a little nearer the opening through which Kazan passed from the windfall into the big world outside. Finally came the time when he reached the opening and crouched there, blinking and frightened at what he saw, and now Gray Wolf no longer tried to hold him back but went out into the sunshine and tried to call him to her. It was three days before his weak eyes had grown strong enough to permit his following her, and very quickly after that Ba-ree learned to love the sun, the warm air, and the sweetness of life, and to dread the darkness of the closed-in den where he had been born.

That this world was not altogether so nice as it at first appeared he was very soon to learn. At the darkening signs of an approaching storm one day Gray Wolf tried to lure him back under the windfall. It was her first warning to Ba-ree and he did not understand. Where Gray Wolf failed, nature came to teach a first lesson. Ba-ree was caught in a sudden deluge of rain. It flattened him out in pure terror and he was drenched and half drowned before Gray Wolf caught him between her jaws and carried him into shelter. One by one after this the first strange

JAMES OLIVER CURWOOD

experiences of life came to him, and one by one his instincts received their birth. Greatest for him of the days to follow was that on which his inquisitive nose touched the raw flesh of a freshly killed and bleeding rabbit. It was his first taste of blood. It was sweet. It filled him with a strange excitement and thereafter he knew what it meant when Kazan brought in something between his jaws. He soon began to battle with sticks in place of the soft fur and his teeth grew as hard and as sharp as little needles.

The Great Mystery was bared to him at last when Kazan brought in between his jaws, a big rabbit that was still alive but so badly crushed that it could not run when dropped to the ground. Ba-ree had learned to know what rabbits and partridges meant—the sweet warm blood that he loved better even than he had ever loved his mother's milk. But they had come to him dead. He had never seen one of the monsters alive. And now the rabbit that Kazan dropped to the ground, kicking and struggling with a broken back, sent Ba-ree back appalled. For a few moments he wonderingly watched the dying throes of Kazan's prey. Both Kazan and Gray Wolf seemed to understand that this was to be Ba-ree's first lesson in his education as a slaying and flesh-eating creature, and they stood close over the rabbit, making no effort to end its struggles. Half a dozen times Gray Wolf sniffed at the rabbit and then turned her blind face toward Ba-ree. After the third or fourth time Kazan stretched himself out on his belly a few feet away and watched the proceedings attentively. Each time that Gray Wolf lowered her head to muzzle the rabbit Ba-ree's little ears shot up expectantly. When he saw that nothing happened and that his mother was not hurt he came a little nearer. Soon he could reach out, stiff-legged and cautious, and touch the furry thing that was not yet dead.

In a last spasmodic convulsion the big rabbit doubled up its rear legs and gave a kick that sent Ba-ree sprawling back, yelping in terror. He regained his feet and then, for the first time, anger and the desire to retaliate took possession of him. The kick had completed his first education. He came back with less caution, but stiffer-legged, and a moment later had dug his tiny teeth in the rabbit's neck. He could feel the throb of life in the soft body, the muscles of the dying rabbit twitched convulsively under him, and he hung with his teeth until there was no longer a tremor of life in his first kill. Gray Wolf was delighted. She caressed Ba-ree with her tongue, and even Kazan condescended to sniff approvingly of his son when he returned to the rabbit. And never before had warm sweet blood tasted so good to Ba-ree as it did to-day.

Swiftly Ba-ree developed from a blood-tasting into a flesh-eating animal. One by one the mysteries of life were unfolded to him—the mating-night chortle of the gray owl, the crash of a falling tree, the roll of thunder, the rush of running water, the scream of a fisher-cat, the mooing of the cow moose, and the distant call of his tribe. But chief of all these mysteries that were already becoming a part of his instinct was the mystery of scent. One day he wandered fifty yards away from the windfall and his little nose touched the warm scent of a rabbit. Instantly, without reasoning or further process of education, he knew that to get at the sweet flesh and blood which he loved he must follow the scent. He wriggled slowly along the trail until he came to a big log, over which the rabbit had vaulted in a long leap, and from this log he turned back. Each day after this he went on adventures of his own. At first he was like an explorer without a compass in a vast and unknown world. Each day he encountered something new, always wonderful, frequently terrifying. But his terrors grew less and less and his confidence correspondingly greater. As he found that none of the things he feared did him any harm he became more and more bold in his investigations. And his appearance was changing, as well as his view of things. His round roly-poly body was taking a different form. He became lithe and quick. The yellow of his coat darkened, and there was a whitish-gray streak along his back like that along Kazan's. He had his mother's under-throat and her beautiful grace of head. Otherwise he was a true son of Kazan. His limbs gave signs of future strength and massiveness. He was broad across the chest. His eyes were wide apart, with a little red in the lower corners. The forest people know what to expect of husky pups who early develop that drop of red. It is a warning that they are born of the wild and that their mothers, or fathers, are of the savage hunt-packs. In Ba-ree that tinge of red was so pronounced that it could mean but one thing. While he was almost half dog, the wild had claimed him forever.

Not until the day of his first real battle with a living creature did Ba-ree come fully into his inheritance. He had gone farther than usual from the windfall—fully a hundred yards. Here he found a new wonder. It was the creek. He had heard it before and he had looked down on it from afar—from a distance of fifty yards at least. But to-day he ventured going to the edge of it, and there he stood for a long time, with the water rippling and singing at his feet, gazing across it into the new world that he saw. Then he moved cautiously along the stream. He had not gone a dozen steps when there was a furious fluttering close to him, and one of the fierce big-eyed jays of the Northland was directly in his path. It could not fly. One of its wings dragged, probably broken in a struggle with some one of the smaller preying beasts. But for an instant it was a most startling and defiant bit of life to Ba-ree.

Then the grayish crest along his back stiffened and he advanced. The wounded jay remained motionless until Ba-ree was within three feet of it. In short quick hops it began to retreat. Instantly Ba-ree's indecision had flown to the four winds. With one sharp excited yelp he flew at the defiant bird. For a few moments there was a thrilling race, and Ba-ree's sharp little teeth buried themselves in the jay's feathers. Swift as a flash the bird's beak began to strike. The jay was the king of the smaller birds. In nesting season it killed the brush sparrows, the mild-eyed moose-birds, and the tree-sappers. Again and again it struck Ba-ree with its powerful beak, but the son of Kazan had now reached the age of battle and the pain of the blows only made his own teeth sink deeper. At last he found the flesh; and a puppyish snarl rose in his throat. Fortunately he had gained a hold under the wing and after the first dozen blows the jay's resistance grew weaker. Five minutes later Ba-ree loosened his teeth and drew back a step to look at the crumpled and motionless creature before him. The jay was dead. He had won his first battle. And with victory came the wonderful dawning of that greatest instinct of all, which told him that no longer was he a drone in the marvelous mechanism of wilderness life—but a part of it from this time forth. *For he had killed*.

Half an hour later Gray Wolf came down over his trail. The jay was torn into bits. Its feathers were scattered about and Ba-ree's little nose was bloody. Ba-ree was lying in triumph beside his victim. Swiftly Gray Wolf understood and caressed him joyously. When they returned to the windfall Ba-ree carried in his jaws what was left of the jay.

From that hour of his first kill hunting became the chief passion of Ba-ree's life. When he was not sleeping in the sun, or under the windfall at night, he was seeking life that he could destroy. He slaughtered an entire family of wood-mice. Moose-birds were at first the easiest for him to stalk, and he killed three. Then he encountered an ermine and the fierce little white outlaw of the forests gave him his first defeat. Defeat cooled his ardor for a few days, but taught him the great lesson that there were other fanged and flesh-eating animals besides himself and that nature had so schemed things that fang must not prey upon fang—*for food*. Many things had been born in him. Instinctively he shunned the porcupine without experiencing the torture of its quills. He came face to face with a fisher-cat one day, a fortnight after his fight with the ermine. Both were seeking food, and as there was no food between them to fight over, each went his own way.

Farther and farther Ba-ree ventured from the windfall, always following the creek. Sometimes he was gone for hours. At first Gray Wolf was restless when he was away, but she seldom went with him and after a time her restlessness left her. Nature was working swiftly. It was Kazan who was restless now. Moonlight nights had come and the wanderlust was growing more and more insistent in his veins. And Gray Wolf, too, was filled with the strange longing to roam at large out into the big world.

Came then the afternoon when Ba-ree went on his longest hunt. Half a mile away he killed his first rabbit. He remained beside it until dusk. The moon rose, big and golden, flooding the forests and plains and ridges with a light almost like that of day. It was a glorious night. And Ba-ree found the moon, and left his kill. And the direction in which he traveled *was away from the windfall*.

All that night Gray Wolf watched and waited. And when at last the moon was sinking into the south and west she settled back on her haunches, turned her blind face to the sky and sent forth her first howl since the day Ba-ree was born. Nature had come into her own. Far away Ba-ree heard, but he did not answer. A new world was his. He had said good-by to the windfall—and home.

XIX

The Usurpers

It was that glorious season between spring and summer, when the northern nights were brilliant with moon and stars, that Kazan and Gray Wolf set up the valley between the two ridges on a long hunt. It was the beginning of that *wanderlust* which always comes to the furred and padded creatures of the wilderness immediately after the young-born of early spring have left their mothers to find their own way in the big world. They struck west from their winter home under the windfall in the swamp. They hunted mostly at night and behind them they left a trail marked by the partly eaten carcasses of rabbits and partridges. It was the season of slaughter and not of hunger. Ten miles west of the swamp they killed a fawn. This, too, they left after a single meal. Their appetites became satiated with warm flesh and blood. They grew sleek and fat and each day they basked longer in the warm sunshine. They had few rivals. The lynxes were in the heavier timber to the south. There were no wolves. Fisher-cat, marten and mink were numerous along the creek, but these were neither swift-hunting nor long-fanged. One day they came upon an old otter. He was a giant of his kind, turning a whitish gray with the approach of summer. Kazan, grown fat and lazy, watched him idly. Blind Gray Wolf sniffed at the fishy smell of him in the air. To them he was no more than a floating stick, a creature out of their element, along with the fish, and they continued on their way not knowing that this uncanny creature with the coal-like flappers was soon to become their ally in one of the strange and deadly feuds of the wilderness, which are as sanguinary to animal life as the deadliest feuds of men are to human life.

The day following their meeting with the otter Gray Wolf and Kazan continued three miles farther westward, still following the stream. Here they encountered the interruption to their progress which turned them over the northward ridge. The obstacle was a huge beaver dam. The dam was two hundred yards in width and flooded a mile of swamp and timber above it. Neither Gray Wolf nor Kazan was deeply interested in beavers. They also moved out of their element, along with the fish and the otter and swift-winged birds.

So they turned into the north, not knowing that nature had already schemed that they four—the dog, wolf, otter and beaver—should soon be engaged in one of those merciless struggles of the wild which keep animal life down to the survival of the fittest, and whose tragic histories are kept secret under the stars and the moon and the winds that tell no tales.

For many years no man had come into this valley between the two ridges to molest the beaver. If a Sarcee trapper had followed down the nameless creek and had caught the patriarch and chief of the colony, he would at once have judged him to be very old and his Indian tongue would have given him a name. He would have called him Broken Tooth, because one of the four long teeth with which he felled trees and built dams was broken off. Six years before Broken Tooth had led a few beavers of his own age down the stream, and they had built their first small dam and their first lodge. The following April Broken Tooth's mate had four little baby beavers, and each of the other mothers in the colony increased the population by two or three or four. At the end of the fourth year this first generation of children, had they followed the usual law of nature, would have mated and left the colony to build a dam and lodges of their own. They mated, but did not emigrate.

The next year the second generation of children, now four years old, mated but did not leave, so that in this early summer of the sixth year the colony was very much like a great city that had been long besieged by an enemy. It numbered fifteen lodges and over a hundred beavers, not counting the fourth babies which had been born during March and April. The dam had been lengthened until it was fully two hundred yards in length. Water had been made to flood large areas of birch and poplar and tangled swamps of tender willow and elder. Even with this food was growing scarce and the lodges were overcrowded. This was because beavers are almost human in their love for home. Broken Tooth's lodge was fully nine feet long by seven wide inside, and there were now living in it children and grandchildren to the number of twenty-seven. For this reason Broken Tooth was preparing to break the precedent of his tribe. When Kazan and Gray Wolf sniffed carelessly at the strong scents of the beaver city, Broken Tooth was marshaling his family, and two of his sons and their families, for the exodus.

As yet Broken Tooth was the recognized leader in the colony. No other beaver had grown to his size and strength. His thick body was fully three feet long. He weighed at least sixty pounds. His tail was fourteen inches in length and five in width, and on a still night he could strike the water a blow that could be heard a quarter of a mile away. His webbed hindfeet were twice as large as his mate's and he was easily the swiftest swimmer in the colony.

Following the afternoon when Gray Wolf and Kazan struck into the north came the clear still night when Broken Tooth climbed to the top of the dam, shook himself, and looked down to see that his army was behind him. The starlit water of the big pond rippled and flashed with the movement of many bodies. A few of the older beavers clambered up after Broken Tooth and the old patriarch plunged down into the narrow stream on the other side of the dam. Now the shining silken bodies of the emigrants followed him in the starlight. In ones and twos and threes they climbed over the dam and with them went a dozen children born three months before. Easily and swiftly they began the journey down-stream, the youngsters swimming furiously to keep up with their parents. In all they numbered forty. Broken Tooth swam well in the lead, with his older workers and battlers behind him. In the rear followed mothers and children.

All of that night the journey continued. The otter, their deadliest enemy—deadlier even than man—hid himself in a thick clump of willows as they passed. Nature, which sometimes sees beyond the vision of man, had made him the enemy of these creatures that were passing his hiding-place in the night. A fish-feeder, he was born to be a conserver as well as a destroyer of the creatures on which he fed Perhaps nature told him that too many beaver dams stopped the run of spawning fish and that where there were many beavers there were always few fish. Maybe he reasoned as to why fish-hunting was poor and he went hungry. So, unable to cope singly with whole tribes of his enemies, he worked to destroy their dams. How this, in turn, destroyed the beavers will be seen in the feud in which nature had already schemed that he should play a part with Kazan and Gray Wolf.

A dozen times during this night Broken Tooth halted to investigate the food supplies along the banks. But in the two or three places where he found plenty of the bark on which they lived it would have been difficult to have constructed a dam. His wonderful engineering instincts rose even above food instincts. And when each time he moved onward, no beaver questioned his judgment by remaining behind. In the early dawn they crossed the burn and came to the edge of the swamp domain of Kazan and Gray Wolf. By right of discovery and possession that swamp belonged to the dog and the wolf. In every part of it they had left their mark of ownership. But Broken Tooth was a creature of the water and the scent of his tribe was not keen. He led on, traveling more slowly when they entered the timber. Just below the windfall home of Kazan and Gray Wolf he halted, and clambering ashore balanced himself upright on his webbed hindfeet and broad four-pound tail. Here he had found ideal conditions. A dam could be constructed easily across the narrow stream, and the water could be made to flood a big supply of poplar, birch, willow and alder. Also the place was sheltered by heavy timber, so that the winters would be warm. Broken Tooth quickly gave his followers to understand that this was to be their new home. On both sides of the stream they swarmed into the near-by timber. The babies began at once to nibble hungrily at the tender bark of willow and alder. The older ones, every one of them now a working engineer, investigated excitedly, breakfasting by nibbling off a mouthful of bark now and then.

That day the work of home-building began. Broken Tooth himself selected a big birch that leaned over the stream, and began the work of cutting through the ten-inch butt with his three long teeth. Though the old patriarch had lost one tooth, the three that remained had not deteriorated with age. The outer edge of them was formed of the hardest enamel; the inner side was of soft ivory. They were like the finest steel chisels, the enamel never wearing away and the softer ivory replacing itself year by year as it was consumed. Sitting on his hindlegs, with his forepaws resting against the tree and with his heavy tail giving him a firm balance, Broken Tooth began gnawing a narrow ring entirely around the tree. He worked tirelessly for several hours, and when at last he stopped to rest another workman took up the task. Meanwhile a dozen beavers were hard at work cutting timber. Long before Broken Tooth's tree was ready to fall across the stream, a smaller poplar crashed into the water. The cutting on the big birch was in the shape of an hour-glass. In twenty hours it fell straight across the creek. While the beaver prefers to do most of his work at night he is a day-laborer as well, and Broken Tooth gave his tribe but little rest during the days that followed. With almost human intelligence the little engineers kept at their task. Smaller trees were felled, and these were cut into four or five foot lengths. One by one these lengths were rolled to the stream, the beavers pushing them with their heads and forepaws, and by means of brush and small limbs they were fastened securely against the birch. When

JAMES OLIVER CURWOOD

the framework was completed the wonderful cement construction was begun. In this the beavers were the masters of men. Dynamite was the only force that could hereafter break up what they were building now. Under their cup-like chins the beavers brought from the banks a mixture of mud and fine twigs, carrying from half a pound to a pound at a load and began filling up the framework with it. Their task seemed tremendous, and yet Broken Tooth's engineers could carry a ton of this mud and twig mixture during a day and night. In three days the water was beginning to back, until it rose about the butts of a dozen or more trees and was flooding a small area of brush. This made work easier. From now on materials could be cut in the water and easily floated. While a part of the beaver colony was taking advantage of the water, others were felling trees end to end with the birch, laying the working frame of a dam a hundred feet in width.

They had nearly accomplished this work when one morning Kazan and Gray Wolf returned to the swamp.

XX

A Feud in the Wilderness

A soft wind blowing from the south and east brought the scent of the invaders to Gray Wolf's nose when they were still half a mile away. She gave the warning to Kazan and he, too, found the strange scent in the air. It grew stronger as they advanced. When two hundred yards from the windfall they heard the sudden crash of a falling tree, and stopped. For a full minute they stood tense and listening. Then the silence was broken by a squeaking cry, followed by a splash. Gray Wolf's alert ears fell back and she turned her blind face understandingly toward Kazan. They trotted ahead slowly, approaching the windfall from behind. Not until they had reached the top of the knoll on which it was situated did Kazan begin to see the wonderful change that had taken place during their absence. Astounded, they stood while he stared. There was no longer a little creek below them. Where it had been was a pond that reached almost to the foot of the knoll. It was fully a hundred feet in width and the backwater had flooded the trees and bush for five or six times that distance toward the burn. They had come up quietly and Broken Tooth's dull-scented workers were unaware of their presence. Not fifty feet away Broken Tooth himself was gnawing at the butt of a tree. An equal distance to the right of him four or five of the baby beavers were at play building a miniature dam of mud and tiny twigs. On the opposite side of the pond was a steep bank six or seven feet high, and here a few of the older children—two years old, but still not workmen—were having great fun climbing the bank and using it as a toboggan-slide. It was their splashing that Kazan and Gray Wolf had heard. In a dozen different places the older beavers were at work.

A few weeks before Kazan had looked upon a similar scene when he had returned into the north from Broken Tooth's old home. It had not interested him then. But a quick and thrilling change swept through him now. The beavers had ceased to be mere water animals, uneatable and with an odor that displeased him. They were invaders—and enemies. His fangs bared silently. His crest stiffened like the hair of a brush, and the muscles of his forelegs and shoulders stood out like whipcords. Not a sound came from him as he rushed down upon Broken Tooth. The old beaver was oblivious of danger until Kazan was within twenty feet of him. Naturally slow of movement on land, he stood for an instant stupefied. Then he swung down from the tree as Kazan leaped upon him. Over and over they rolled to the edge of the bank, carried on by the dog's momentum. In another moment the thick heavy body of the beaver had slipped like oil from under Kazan and Broken Tooth was safe in his element, two holes bitten clean through his fleshy tail. Baffled in his effort to get a death-hold on Broken Tooth, Kazan swung like a flash to the right. The young beavers had not moved. Astonished and frightened at what they had seen, they stood as if stupefied. Not until they saw Kazan tearing toward them did they awaken to action. Three of them reached the water. The fourth and fifth—baby beavers not more than three months old—were too late. With a single snap of his jaw Kazan broke the hack of one. The other he pinned down by the throat and shook as a terrier shakes a rat. When Gray Wolf trotted down to him both of the little beavers were dead. She sniffed at their soft little bodies and whined. Perhaps the baby creatures reminded her of runaway Ba-ree, her own baby, for there was a note of longing in her whine as she nosed them. It was the mother whine.

But if Gray Wolf had visions of her own Kazan understood nothing of them. He had killed two of the creatures that had dared to invade their home. To the little beavers he had been as merciless as the gray lynx that had murdered Gray Wolf's first children on the top of the Sun Rock. Now that he had sunk his teeth into the flesh of his enemies his blood was filled with a frenzied desire to kill. He raved along the edge of the pond, snarling at the uneasy water under which Broken Tooth had disappeared. All of the beavers had taken refuge in the pond, and its surface was heaving with the passing of many bodies beneath. Kazan came to the end of the dam. This was new. Instinctively he knew that it was the work of Broken Tooth and his tribe and for a few moments he tore fiercely at the matted sticks and limbs. Suddenly there was an upheaval of water close to the dam, fifty feet out from the bank, and Broken Tooth's big gray head appeared. For a tense half minute Broken Tooth and Kazan measured each other at that distance. Then Broken Tooth drew his wet shining body out of the water to the top of the dam, and squatted flat, facing Kazan. The old patriarch was alone. Not another beaver had shown himself.

The surface of the pond had now become quiet. Vainly Kazan tried to discover a footing that would allow him to reach the watchful invader. But between the solid wall of the dam and the bank there was a tangled framework through which the water rushed with some violence. Three times Kazan fought to work his way through that tangle, and three times his efforts ended in sudden plunges into the water. All this time Broken Tooth did not move. When at last Kazan gave up the attack the old engineer slipped over the edge of the dam and disappeared under the water. He had learned that Kazan, like the lynx, could not fight water and he spread the news among the members of his colony.

Gray Wolf and Kazan returned to the windfall and lay down in the warm sun. Half an hour later Broken Tooth drew himself out on the opposite shore of the pond. He was followed by other beavers. Across the water they resumed their work as if nothing had happened. The tree-cutters returned to their trees. Half a dozen worked in the water, carrying loads of cement and twigs. The middle of the pond was their dead-line. Across this not one of them passed. A dozen times during the hour that followed one of the beavers swam up to the dead-line, and rested there, looking at the shining little bodies of the babies that Kazan had killed. Perhaps it was the mother, and perhaps some finer instinct unknown to Kazan told this to Gray Wolf. For Gray Wolf went down twice to sniff at the dead bodies, and each time—without seeing—she went when the mother beaver had come to the dead-line.

The first fierce animus had worn itself from Kazan's blood, and he now watched the beavers closely. He had learned that they were not fighters. They were many to one and yet they ran from him like a lot of rabbits. Broken Tooth had not even struck at him, and slowly it grew upon him that these invading creatures that used both the water and land would have to be hunted as he stalked the rabbit and the partridge. Early in the afternoon he slipped off into the bush, followed by Gray Wolf. He had often begun the stalking of a rabbit by moving *away* from it and he employed this wolf trick now with the beavers. Beyond the windfall he turned and began trotting up the creek, with the wind. For a quarter of a mile the creek was deeper than it had ever been. One of their old fording places was completely submerged, and at last Kazan plunged in and swam across, leaving Gray Wolf to wait for him on the windfall side of the stream.

Alone he made his way quickly in the direction of the dam, traveling two hundred yards back from the creek. Twenty yards below the dam a dense thicket of alder and willow grew close to the creek and Kazan took advantage of this. He approached within a leap or two of the dam without being seen and crouched close to the ground, ready to spring forth when the opportunity came. Most of the beavers were now working in the water. The four or five still on shore were close to the water and some distance up-stream. After a wait of several minutes Kazan was almost on the point of staking everything on a wild rush upon his enemies when a movement on the dam attracted his attention. Half-way out two or three beavers were at work strengthening the central structure with cement. Swift as a flash Kazan darted from his cover to the shelter behind the dam. Here the water was very shallow, the main portion of the stream finding a passage close to the opposite shore. Nowhere did it reach to his belly as he waded out. He was completely hidden from the beavers, and the wind was in his favor. The noise of running water drowned what little sound he made. Soon he heard the beaver workmen over him. The branches of the fallen birch gave him a footing, and he clambered up.

A moment later his head and shoulders appeared above the top of the dam. Scarce an arm's length away Broken Tooth was forcing into place a three-foot length of poplar as big around as a man's arm. He was so busy that he did not hear or see Kazan. Another beaver gave the warning as he plunged into the pond. Broken Tooth looked up, and his eyes met Kazan's bared fangs. There was no time to turn. He threw himself back, but it was a moment too late. Kazan was upon him. His long fangs sank deep into Broken Tooth's neck. But the old beaver had thrown himself enough back to make Kazan lose his footing. At the same moment his chisel-like teeth got a firm hold of the loose skin at Kazan's throat. Thus clinched, with Kazan's long teeth buried almost to the beaver's jugular, they plunged down into the deep water of the pond.

Broken Tooth weighed sixty pounds. The instant he struck the water he was in his element, and holding tenaciously to the grip he had obtained on Kazan's neck he sank like a chunk of iron. Kazan was pulled completely under. The water rushed into his mouth, his ears, eyes and nose. He was blinded, and his senses were a roaring tumult. But instead of struggling to free himself he held his breath and buried his teeth deeper. They touched the soft bottom and for a moment floundered in the mud. Then Kazan loosened his hold. He was fighting for his own life now—and not for Broken Tooth's. With all of the strength of his powerful limbs he struggled to break loose—to rise to the surface, to fresh air, to life. He clamped his jaws shut, knowing that to breathe was to die. On land he could have freed himself from Broken Tooth's hold without an effort. But under water the old beaver's grip was more deadly than would have been the fangs of a lynx ashore. There was a sudden swirl of water as a second beaver circled close about the struggling pair. Had he closed in with Broken Tooth, Kazan's struggles would quickly have ceased.

But nature had not foreseen the day when Broken Tooth would be fighting with fang. The old patriarch had no particular reason now for holding Kazan down. He was not vengeful. He did not thirst for blood or death. Finding that he was free, and that this strange enemy that had twice leaped upon him could do him no harm, he loosed his hold. It was not a moment too soon for Kazan. He was struggling weakly when he rose to the surface of the water. Three-quarters drowned, he succeeded in raising his forepaws over a slender branch that projected from the dam. This gave him time to fill his lungs with air, and to cough forth the water that had almost ended his existence. For ten minutes he clung to the branch before he dared attempt the short swim ashore. When he reached the bank he dragged himself up weakly. All the strength was gone from his body. His limbs shook. His jaws hung loose. He was beaten—completely beaten. And a creature without a fang had worsted him. He felt the abasement of it. Drenched and slinking, he went to the windfall, lay down in the sun, and waited for Gray Wolf.

Days followed in which Kazan's desire to destroy his beaver enemies became the consuming passion of his life. Each day the dam became more formidable. Cement work in the water was carried on by the beavers swiftly and safely. The water in the pond rose higher each twenty-four hours, and the pond grew steadily wider. The water had now been turned into the depression that encircled the windfall, and in another week or two, if the beavers continued their work, Kazan's and Gray Wolf's home would be nothing more than a small island in the center of a wide area of submerged swamp.

Kazan hunted only for food now, and not for pleasure. Ceaselessly he watched his opportunity to leap upon incautious members of Broken Tooth's tribe. The third day after the struggle under the water he killed a big beaver that approached too close to the willow thicket. The fifth day two of the young beavers wandered into the flooded depression back of the windfall and Kazan caught them in shallow water and tore them into pieces. After these successful assaults the beavers began to work mostly at night. This was to Kazan's advantage, for he was a night-hunter. On each of two consecutive nights he killed a beaver. Counting the young, he had killed seven when the otter came.

Never had Broken Tooth been placed between two deadlier or more ferocious enemies than the two that now assailed him. On shore Kazan was his master because of his swiftness, keener scent, and fighting trickery. In the water the otter was a still greater menace. He was swifter than the fish that he caught for food. His teeth were like steel needles. He was so sleek and slippery that it would have been impossible for them to hold him with their chisel-like teeth could they have caught him. The otter, like the beaver, possessed no hunger for blood. Yet in all the Northland he was the greatest destroyer of their kind—an even greater destroyer than man. He came and passed like a plague, and it was in the coldest days of winter that greatest destruction came with him. In those days he did not assault the beavers in their snug houses. He did what man could do only with dynamite—made an embrasure through their dam. Swiftly the water would fall, the surface ice would crash down, and the beaver houses would be left out of water. Then followed death for the beavers—starvation and cold. With the protecting water gone from about their houses, the drained pond a chaotic mass of broken ice, and the temperature forty or fifty degrees below zero, they would die within a few hours. For the beaver, with his thick coat of fur, can stand less cold than man. Through all the long winter the water about his home is as necessary to him as fire to a child.

But it was summer now and Broken Tooth and his colony had no very great fear of the otter. It would cost them some labor to repair the damage he did, but there was plenty of food and it was warm. For two days the otter frisked about the dam and the deep water of the pond. Kazan took him for a beaver, and tried vainly to stalk him. The otter regarded Kazan suspiciously and kept well out of his way. Neither knew that the other was an ally. Meanwhile the beavers continued their work with greater caution. The water in the pond had now risen to a point where the engineers had begun the construction of three lodges. On the third day the destructive instinct of the otter began its work. He began to examine the dam, close down to the foundation. It was not long before he found a weak spot to begin work on, and with his sharp teeth and small bullet-like head he commenced his drilling operations. Inch by inch he worked his way through the dam, burrowing and gnawing over and under the timbers, and always through the cement. The round hole he made was fully seven inches in diameter. In six hours he had cut it through the five-foot base of the dam.

A torrent of water began to rush from the pond as if forced out by a hydraulic pump. Kazan and Gray Wolf were hiding in the willows on the south side of the pond when this happened. They heard the roar of the stream tearing through the embrasure and Kazan saw the otter crawl up to the top of the dam and shake himself like a huge water-rat. Within thirty minutes the water in the pond had fallen perceptibly, and the force of the water pouring through the hole was constantly increasing the outlet. In another half hour the foundations of the three lodges, which had been laid in about ten inches of water, stood on mud. Not until Broken Tooth discovered that the water was receding from the houses did he take alarm. He was thrown into a panic, and very soon every beaver in the colony tearing excitedly about the pond. They swam swiftly from shore to shore, paying no attention to the dead-line now. Broken Tooth and the older workmen made for the dam, and with a snarling cry the otter plunged down among them and out like a flash for the creek above the pond. Swiftly the water continued to fall and as it fell the excitement of the beavers increased. They forgot Kazan and Gray Wolf.

Several of the younger members of the colony drew themselves ashore on the windfall side of the pond, and whining softly Kazan was about to slip back through the willows when one of the older beavers waddled up through the deepening mud close on his ambush. In two leaps Kazan was upon him, with Gray Wolf a leap behind him. The short fierce struggle in the mud was seen by the other beavers and they crossed swiftly to the opposite side of the pond. The water had receded to a half of its greatest width before Broken Tooth and his workmen discovered the breach in the wall of the dam. The work of repair was begun at once. For this work sticks and brush of considerable size were necessary, and to reach this material the beavers were compelled to drag their heavy bodies through the ten or fifteen yards of soft mud left by the falling water. Peril of fang no longer kept them back. Instinct told them that they were fighting for their existence—that if the embrasure were not filled up and the water kept in the pond they would very soon be completely exposed to their enemies. It was a day of slaughter for Gray Wolf and Kazan. They killed two more beavers in the mud close to the willows. Then they crossed the creek below the dam and cut off three beavers in the depression behind the windfall. There was no escape for these three. They were torn into pieces. Farther up the creek Kazan caught a young beaver and killed it.

Late in the afternoon the slaughter ended. Broken Tooth and his courageous engineers had at last repaired the breach, and the water in the pond began to rise.

Half a mile up the creek the big otter was squatted on a log basking in the last glow of the setting sun. To-morrow he would go and do over again his work of destruction. That was his method. For him it was play.

But that strange and unseen arbiter of the forests called O-ee-ki, "the Spirit," by those who speak the wild tongue, looked down at last with mercy upon Broken Tooth and his death-stricken tribe. For in that last glow of sunset Kazan and Gray Wolf slipped stealthily up the creek—to find the otter basking half asleep on the log.

The day's work, a full stomach, and the pool of warm sunlight in which he lay had all combined to make the otter sleepy. He was as motionless as the log on which he had stretched himself. He was big and gray and old. For ten years he had lived to prove his cunning superior to that of man. Vainly traps had been set for him. Wily trappers had built narrow sluice-ways of rock and tree in small streams for him, but the old otter had foiled their cunning and escaped the steel jaws waiting at the lower end of each sluice. The trail he left in soft mud told of his size. A few trappers had seen him. His soft pelt would long ago have found its way to London, Paris or Berlin had it not been for his cunning. He was fit for a princess, a duke or an emperor. For ten years he had lived and escaped the demands of the rich.

But this was summer. No trapper would have killed him now, for his pelt was worthless. Nature and instinct both told him this. At this season he did not dread man, for there was no man to dread. So he lay asleep on the log, oblivious to everything but the comfort of sleep and the warmth of the sun.

Soft-footed, searching still for signs of the furry enemies who had invaded their domain, Kazan slipped along the creek. Gray Wolf ran close at his shoulder. They made no sound, and the wind was in their favor—bringing scents toward them. It brought the otter smell. To Kazan and Gray Wolf it was the scent of a water animal, rank and fishy, and they took it for the beaver. They advanced still more cautiously. Then Kazan saw the big otter asleep on the log and he gave the warning to Gray Wolf. She stopped, standing with her head thrown up, while Kazan made his stealthy advance. The otter stirred uneasily. It was growing dusk. The golden pool of sunlight had faded away. Back in the darkening timber an owl greeted night with its first-low call. The otter breathed deeply. His whiskered muzzle twitched. He was awakening—stirring—when Kazan leaped upon him. Face to face, in fair fight, the old otter could have given a good account of himself. But there was no chance now. The wild itself had for the first time in his life become his deadliest enemy. It was not man now—but O-ee-ki, "the Spirit," that had laid its hand upon him. And from the Spirit there was no escape. Kazan's fangs sank into his soft jugular. Perhaps he died without knowing what it was that had leaped upon him. For he died—quickly, and Kazan and Gray Wolf went on their way, hunting still for enemies to slaughter, and not knowing that in the otter they had killed the one ally who would have driven the beavers from their swamp home.

The days that followed grew more and more hopeless for Kazan and Gray Wolf. With the otter gone Broken Tooth and his tribe held the winning hand. Each day the water backed a little farther into the depression surrounding the windfall. By the middle of July only a narrow strip of land connected the windfall hummock with the dry land of the swamp. In deep water the beavers now worked unmolested. Inch by inch the water rose, until there came the day when it began to overflow the connecting strip. For the last time Kazan and Gray Wolf passed from their windfall home and traveled up the stream between the two ridges. The creek held a new meaning for them now and as they traveled they sniffed its odors and listened to its sounds with an interest they had never known before. It was an interest mingled a little with fear, for something in the manner in which the beavers had beaten them reminded Kazan and Gray Wolf of *man*. And that night, when in the radiance of the big white moon they came within scent of the beaver colony that Broken Tooth had left, they turned quickly northward into the plains. Thus had brave old Broken Tooth taught them to respect the flesh and blood and handiwork of his tribe.

XXI

A Shot on the Sand-Bar

July and August of 1911 were months of great fires in the Northland. The swamp home of Kazan and Gray Wolf, and the green valley between the two ridges, had escaped the seas of devastating flame; but now, as they set forth on their wandering adventures again, it was not long before their padded feet came in contact with the seared and blackened desolation that had followed so closely after the plague and starvation of the preceding winter. In his humiliation and defeat, after being driven from his swamp home by the beavers, Kazan led his blind mate first into the south. Twenty miles beyond the ridge they struck the fire-killed forests. Winds from Hudson's Bay had driven the flames in an unbroken sea into the west, and they had left not a vestige of life or a patch of green. Blind Gray Wolf could not see the blackened world, but she *sensed* it. It recalled to her memory of that other fire, after the battle on the Sun Rock; and all of her wonderful instincts, sharpened and developed by her blindness, told her that to the north—and not south—lay the hunting-grounds they were seeking. The strain of dog that was in Kazan still pulled him south. It was not because he sought man, for to man he had now become as deadly an enemy as Gray Wolf herself. It was simply dog instinct to travel southward; in the face of fire it was wolf instinct to travel northward. At the end of the third day Gray Wolf won. They recrossed the little valley between the two ridges, and swung north and west into the Athabasca country, striking a course that would ultimately bring them to the headwaters of the McFarlane River.

Late in the preceding autumn a prospector had come up to Fort Smith, on the Slave River, with a pickle bottle filled with gold dust and nuggets. He had made the find on the McFarlane. The first mails had taken the news to the outside world, and by midwinter the earliest members of a treasure-hunting horde were rushing into the country by snow-shoe and dog-sledge. Other finds came thick and fast. The McFarlane was rich in free gold, and miners by the score staked out their claims along it and began work. Latecomers swung to new fields farther north and east, and to Fort Smith came rumors of "finds" richer than those of the Yukon. A score of men at first—then a hundred, five hundred, a thousand—rushed into the new country. Most of these were from the prairie countries to the south, and from the placer beds of the Saskatchewan and the Frazer. From the far North, traveling by way of the Mackenzie and the Liard, came a smaller number of seasoned prospectors and adventurers from the Yukon—men who knew what it meant to starve and freeze and die by inches.

One of these late comers was Sandy McTrigger. There were several reasons why Sandy had left the Yukon. He was "in bad" with the police who patrolled the country west of Dawson, and he was "broke." In spite of these facts he was one of the best prospectors that had ever followed the shores of the Klondike. He had made discoveries running up to a million or two, and had promptly lost them through gambling and drink. He had no conscience, and little fear. Brutality was the chief thing written in his face. His undershot jaw, his wide eyes, low forehead and grizzly mop of red hair proclaimed him at once as a man not to be trusted beyond one's own vision or the reach of a bullet. It was suspected that he had killed a couple of men, and robbed others, but as yet the police had failed to get anything "on" him. But along with this bad side of him, Sandy McTrigger possessed a coolness and a courage which even his worst enemies could not but admire, and also certain mental depths which his unpleasant features did not proclaim.

Inside of six months Red Gold City had sprung up on the McFarlane, a hundred and fifty miles from Fort Smith, and Fort Smith was five hundred miles from civilization. When Sandy came he looked over the crude collection of shacks, gambling houses and saloons in the new town, and made up his mind that the time was not ripe for any of his "inside" schemes just yet. He gambled a little, and won sufficient to buy himself grub and half an outfit. A feature of this outfit was an old muzzle-loading rifle. Sandy, who always carried the latest Savage on the market, laughed at it. But it was the best his finances would allow of. He started south—up the McFarlane. Beyond a certain point on the river prospectors had found no gold. Sandy pushed confidently *beyond* this point. Not until he was in new country did he begin his search. Slowly he worked his way up a small tributary whose headwaters were fifty or sixty miles to the south and east. Here and there he found fairly good placer gold. He might have panned six or eight dollars' worth a day. With this much he was disgusted. Week after week he continued to work his way up-stream, and the farther he went the poorer his pans became. At last only occasionally did he find colors. After such

JAMES OLIVER CURWOOD

disgusting weeks as these Sandy was dangerous—when in the compa_
of others. Alone he was harmless.

One afternoon he ran his canoe ashore on a white strip of sand. This
was at a bend, where the stream had widened, and gave promise of at
least a few colors. He had bent down close to the edge of the water
when something caught his attention on the wet sand. What he saw
were the footprints of animals. Two had come down to drink. They had
stood side by side. And the footprints were fresh—made not more than
an hour or two before. A gleam of interest shot into Sandy's eyes. He
looked behind him, and up and down the stream.

"Wolves," he grunted. "Wish I could 'a' shot at 'em with that old
minute-gun back there. Gawd—listen to that! And in broad daylight,
too!"

He jumped to his feet, staring off into the bush.

A quarter of a mile away Gray Wolf had caught the dreaded scent
of man in the wind, and was giving voice to her warning. It was a long
wailing howl, and not until its last echoes had died away did Sandy
McTrigger move. Then he returned to the canoe, took out his old gun,
put a fresh cap on the nipple and disappeared quickly over the edge of
the bank.

For a week Kazan and Gray Wolf had been wandering about the
headwaters of the McFarlane and this was the first time since the
preceding winter that Gray Wolf had caught the scent of man in the air.
When the wind brought the danger-signal to her she was alone. Two
or three minutes before the scent came to her Kazan had left her side
in swift pursuit of a snow-shoe rabbit, and she lay flat on her belly
under a bush, waiting for him. In these moments when she was alone
Gray Wolf was constantly sniffing the air. Blindness had developed her
scent and hearing until they were next to infallible. First she had heard
the rattle of Sandy McTrigger's paddle against the side of his canoe a
quarter of a mile away. Scent had followed swiftly. Five minutes after
her warning howl Kazan stood at her side, his head flung up, his jaws
open and panting. Sandy had hunted Arctic foxes, and he was using the
Eskimo tactics now, swinging in a half-circle until he should come up in
the face of the wind. Kazan caught a single whiff of the man-tainted air
and his spine grew stiff. But blind Gray Wolf was keener than the little
red-eyed fox of the North. Her pointed nose slowly followed Sandy's
progress. She heard a dry stick crack under his feet three hundred yards
away. She caught the metallic click of his gun-barrel as it struck a birch

pling. The moment she lost Sandy in the wind she whined and rubbed herself against Kazan and trotted a few steps to the southwest.

At times such as this Kazan seldom refused to take guidance from her. They trotted away side by side and by the time Sandy was creeping up snake-like with the wind in his face, Kazan was peering from the fringe of river brush down upon the canoe on the white strip of sand. When Sandy returned, after an hour of futile stalking, two fresh tracks led straight down to the canoe. He looked at them in amazement and then a sinister grin wrinkled his ugly face. He chuckled as he went to his kit and dug out a small rubber bag. From this he drew a tightly corked bottle, filled with gelatine capsules. In each little capsule were five grains of strychnine. There were dark hints that once upon a time Sandy McTrigger had tried one of these capsules by dropping it in a cup of coffee and giving it to a man, but the police had never proved it. He was expert in the use of poison. Probably he had killed a thousand foxes in his time, and he chuckled again as he counted out a dozen of the capsules and thought how easy it would be to get this inquisitive pair of wolves. Two or three days before he had killed a caribou, and each of the capsules he now rolled up in a little ball of deer fat, doing the work with short sticks in place of his fingers, so that there would be no man-smell clinging to the death-baits. Before sundown Sandy set out at right-angles over the plain, planting the baits. Most of them he hung to low bushes. Others he dropped in worn rabbit and caribou trails. Then he returned to the creek and cooked his supper.

Then next morning he was up early, and off to the poison baits. The first bait was untouched. The second was as he had planted it. The third was gone. A thrill shot through Sandy as he looked about him. Somewhere within a radius of two or three hundred yards he would find his game. Then his glance fell to the ground under the bush where he had hung the poison capsule and an oath broke from his lips. The bait had not been eaten. The caribou fat lay scattered under the bush and still imbedded in the largest portion of it was the little white capsule—unbroken. It was Sandy's first experience with a wild creature whose instincts were sharpened by blindness, and he was puzzled. He had never known this to happen before. If a fox or a wolf could be lured to the point of touching a bait, it followed that the bait was eaten. Sandy went on to the fourth and the fifth baits. They were untouched. The sixth was torn to pieces, like the third. In this instance the capsule was broken and the white powder scattered. Two more poison baits Sandy found pulled down in this manner. He knew that Kazan and Gray Wolf had done the work, for he found the marks of their feet in a dozen different places. The accumulated bad humor of weeks of futile labor found vent in his disappointment and anger. At last he had found something tangible to curse. The failure of his poison baits he accepted as a sort of climax to his general bad luck. Everything was against him, he believed, and he made up his mind to return to Red Gold City. Early in the afternoon he launched his canoe and drifted down-stream with the current. He was content to let the current do all of the work to-day, and he used his paddle just enough to keep his slender craft head on. He leaned back comfortably and smoked his pipe, with the old rifle between his knees. The wind was in his face and he kept a sharp watch for game.

It was late in the afternoon when Kazan and Gray Wolf came out on a sand-bar five or six miles down-stream. Kazan was lapping up the cool water when Sandy drifted quietly around a bend a hundred yards above them. If the wind had been right, or if Sandy had been using his paddle, Gray Wolf would have detected danger. It was the metallic click-click of the old-fashioned lock of Sandy's rifle that awakened her to a sense of peril. Instantly she was thrilled by the nearness of it. Kazan heard the sound and stopped drinking to face it. In that moment Sandy pressed the trigger. A belch of smoke, a roar of gunpowder, and Kazan felt a red-hot stream of fire pass with the swiftness of a lightning-flash through his brain. He stumbled back, his legs gave way under him, and he crumpled down in a limp heap. Gray Wolf darted like a streak off into the bush. Blind, she had not seen Kazan wilt down upon the white sand. Not until she was a quarter of a mile away from the terrifying thunder of the white man's rifle did she stop and wait for him.

Sandy McTrigger grounded his canoe on the sand-bar with an exultant yell.

"Got you, you old devil, didn't I?" he cried. "I'd 'a' got the other, too, if I'd 'a' had something besides this damned old relic!"

He turned Kazan's head over with the butt of his gun, and the leer of satisfaction in his face gave place to a sudden look of amazement. For the first time he saw the collar about Kazan's neck.

"My Gawd, it ain't a wolf," he gasped. "It's a dog, Sandy McTrigger—*a dog!*"

XXII

SANDY'S METHOD

McTrigger dropped on his knees in the sand. The look of exultation was gone from his face. He twisted the collar about the dog's limp neck until he came to the worn plate, on which he could make out the faintly engraved letters *K-a-z-a-n*. He spelled the letters out one by one, and the look in his face was of one who still disbelieved what he had seen and heard.

"A dog!" he exclaimed again. "A dog, Sandy McTrigger an' a—a beauty!"

He rose to his feet and looked down on his victim. A pool of blood lay in the white sand at the end of Kazan's nose. After a moment Sandy bent over to see where his bullet had struck. His inspection filled him with a new and greater interest. The heavy ball from the muzzle-loader had struck Kazan fairly on top of the head. It was a glancing blow that had not even broken the skull, and like a flash Sandy understood the quivering and twitching of Kazan's shoulders and legs. He had thought that they were the last muscular throes of death. But Kazan was not dying. He was only stunned, and would be on his feet again in a few minutes. Sandy was a connoisseur of dogs—of dogs that had worn sledge traces. He had lived among them two-thirds of his life. He could tell their age, their value, and a part of their history at a glance. In the snow he could tell the trail of a Mackenzie hound from that of a Malemute, and the track of an Eskimo dog from that of a Yukon husky. He looked at Kazan's feet. They were wolf feet, and he chuckled. Kazan was part wild. He was big and powerful, and Sandy thought of the coming winter, and of the high prices that dogs would bring at Red Gold City. He went to the canoe and returned with a roll of stout moose-hide babiche. Then he sat down cross-legged in front of Kazan and began making a muzzle. He did this by plaiting babiche thongs in the same manner that one does in making the web of a snow-shoe. In ten minutes he had the muzzle over Kazan's nose and fastened securely about his neck. To the dog's collar he then fastened a ten-foot rope of babiche. After that he sat back and waited for Kazan to come to life.

When Kazan first lifted his head he could not see. There was a red film before his eyes. But this passed away swiftly and he saw the man. His first instinct was to rise to his feet. Three times he fell back before he could stand up. Sandy was squatted six feet from him, holding the end of the babiche, and grinning. Kazan's fangs gleamed back. He growled, and the crest along his spine rose menacingly. Sandy jumped to his feet.

"Guess I know what you're figgering on," he said. "I've had *your* kind before. The dam' wolves have turned you bad, an' you'll need a whole lot of club before you're right again. Now, look here."

Sandy had taken the precaution of bringing a thick club along with the babiche. He picked it up from where he had dropped it in the sand. Kazan's strength had fairly returned to him now. He was no longer dizzy. The mist had cleared away from his eyes. Before him he saw once more his old enemy, man—man and the club. All of the wild ferocity of his nature was roused in an instant. Without reasoning he knew that Gray Wolf was gone, and that this man was accountable for her going. He knew that this man had also brought him his own hurt, and what he ascribed to the man he also attributed to the club. In his newer undertaking of things, born of freedom and Gray Wolf, Man and Club were one and inseparable. With a snarl he leaped at Sandy. The man was not expecting a direct assault, and before he could raise his club or spring aside Kazan had landed full on his chest. The muzzle about Kazan's jaws saved him. Fangs that would have torn his throat open snapped harmlessly. Under the weight of the dog's body he fell back, as if struck down by a catapult.

As quick as a cat he was on his feet again, with the end of the babiche twisted several times about his hand. Kazan leaped again, and this time he was met by a furious swing of the club. It smashed against his shoulder, and sent him down in the sand. Before he could recover Sandy was upon him, with all the fury of a man gone mad. He shortened the babiche by twisting it again and again about his hand, and the club rose and fell with the skill and strength of one long accustomed to its use. The first blows served only to add to Kazan's hatred of man, and the ferocity and fearlessness of his attacks. Again and again he leaped in, and each time the club fell upon him with a force that threatened to break his bones. There was a tense hard look about Sandy's cruel mouth. He had never known a dog like this before, and he was a bit nervous, even with Kazan muzzled. Three times Kazan's fangs would have sunk deep in his flesh had it not been for the babiche. And if the thongs about his jaws should slip, or break—.

Sandy followed up the thought with a smashing blow that landed on Kazan's head, and once more the old battler fell limp upon the sand. McTrigger's breath was coming in quick gasps. He was almost winded. Not until the club slipped from his hand did he realize how desperate the fight had been. Before Kazan recovered from the blow that had stunned him Sandy examined the muzzle and strengthened it by adding another babiche thong. Then he dragged Kazan to a log that high water had thrown up on the shore a few yards away and made the end of the babiche rope fast to a dead snag. After that he pulled his canoe higher up on the sand, and began to prepare camp for the night.

For some minutes after Kazan's stunned senses had become normal he lay motionless, watching Sandy McTrigger. Every bone in his body gave him pain. His jaws were sore and bleeding. His upper lip was smashed where the club had fallen. One eye was almost closed. Several times Sandy came near, much pleased at what he regarded as the good results of the beating. Each time he brought the club. The third time he prodded Kazan with it, and the dog snarled and snapped savagely at the end of it. That was what Sandy wanted—it was an old trick of the dog-slaver. Instantly he was using the club again, until with a whining cry Kazan slunk under the protection of the snag to which he was fastened. He could scarcely drag himself. His right forepaw was smashed. His hindquarters sank under him. For a time after this second beating he could not have escaped had he been free.

Sandy was in unusually good humor.

"I'll take the devil out of you all right," he told Kazan for the twentieth time. "There's nothin' like beatin's to make dogs an' wimmin live up to the mark. A month from now you'll be worth two hundred dollars or I'll skin you alive!"

Three or four times before dusk Sandy worked to rouse Kazan's animosity. But there was no longer any desire left in Kazan to fight. His two terrific beatings, and the crushing blow of the bullet against his skull, had made him sick. He lay with his head between his forepaws, his eyes closed, and did not see McTrigger. He paid no attention to the meat that was thrown under his nose. He did not know when the last of the sun sank behind the western forests, or when the darkness came. But at last something roused him from his stupor. To his dazed and sickened brain it came like a call from out of the far past, and he raised his head and listened. Out on the sand McTrigger had built a fire, and the man stood in the red glow of it now, facing the dark shadows beyond the shoreline. He, too, was listening. What had roused Kazan came again now—the lost mourning cry of Gray Wolf far out on the plain.

With a whine Kazan was on his feet, tugging at the babiche. Sandy snatched up his club, and leaped toward him.

"Down, you brute!" he commanded.

In the firelight the club rose and fell with ferocious quickness. When McTrigger returned to the fire he was breathing hard again. He tossed his club beside the blankets he had spread out for a bed. It was a different looking club now. It was covered with blood and hair.

"Guess that'll take the spirit out of him," he chuckled. "It'll do that— or kill 'im!"

Several times that night Kazan heard Gray Wolf's call. He whined softly in response, fearing the club. He watched the fire until the last embers of it died out, and then cautiously dragged himself from under the snag. Two or three times he tried to stand on his feet, but fell back each time. His legs were not broken, but the pain of standing on them was excruciating. He was hot and feverish. All that night he had craved a drink of water. When Sandy crawled out from between his blankets in the early dawn he gave him both meat and water. Kazan drank the water, but would not touch the meat. Sandy regarded the change in him with satisfaction. By the time the sun was up he had finished his breakfast and was ready to leave. He approached Kazan fearlessly now, without the club. Untying the babiche he dragged the dog to the canoe. Kazan slunk in the sand while his captor fastened the end of the hide rope to the stern of the canoe. Sandy grinned. What was about to happen would be fun for him. In the Yukon he had learned how to take the spirit out of dogs.

He pushed off, bow foremost. Bracing himself with his paddle he then began to pull Kazan toward the water. In a few moments Kazan stood with his forefeet planted in the damp sand at the edge of the stream. For a brief interval Sandy allowed the babiche to fall slack. Then with a sudden powerful pull he jerked Kazan out into the water. Instantly he sent the canoe into midstream, swung it quickly down with the current, and began to paddle enough to keep the babiche taut about his victim's neck. In spite of his sickness and injuries Kazan was now compelled to swim to keep his head above water. In the wash of the canoe, and with Sandy's strokes growing steadily stronger, his position became each moment one of increasing torture. At times his shaggy head was pulled completely under water. At others Sandy would wait until he had drifted alongside, and then thrust him under with the end of his paddle. He grew weaker. At the end of a half-mile he was drowning. Not until then did Sandy pull him alongside and drag him into the canoe. The dog fell limp and gasping in the bottom. Brutal though Sandy's methods had been, they had worked his purpose. In Kazan there was no longer a desire to fight. He no longer struggled for freedom. He knew that this man was his master, and for the time his spirit was gone. All he desired now was to be allowed to lie in the bottom of the canoe, out of reach of the club, and safe from the water. The club lay between him and the man. The end of it was within a foot or two of his nose, and what he smelled was his own blood.

For five days and five nights the journey down-stream continued, and McTrigger's process of civilizing Kazan was continued in three more beatings with the club, and another resort to the water torture. On the morning of the sixth day they reached Red Gold City, and McTrigger put up his tent close to the river. Somewhere he obtained a chain for Kazan, and after fastening the dog securely back of the tent he cut off the babiche muzzle.

"You can't put on meat in a muzzle," he told his prisoner. "An' I want you to git strong—an' fierce as hell. I've got an idee. It's an idee you can lick your weight in wildcats. We'll pull off a stunt pretty soon that'll fill our pockets with dust. I've done it afore, and we can do it *here*. Wolf an' dog—s'elp me Gawd but it'll be a drawin' card!"

Twice a day after this he brought fresh raw meat to Kazan. Quickly Kazan's spirit and courage returned to him. The soreness left his limbs. His battered jaws healed. And after the fourth day each time that Sandy came with meat he greeted him with the challenge of his snarling fangs. McTrigger did not beat him now. He gave him no fish, no tallow and meal—nothing but raw meat. He traveled five miles up the river to bring in the fresh entrail of a caribou that had been killed. One day Sandy brought another man with him and when the stranger came a step too near Kazan made a sudden swift lunge at him. The man jumped back with a startled oath.

"He'll do," he growled. "He's lighter by ten or fifteen pounds than the Dane, but he's got the teeth, an' the quickness, an' he'll give a good show before he goes under."

"I'll make you a bet of twenty-five per cent. of my share that he don't go under," offered Sandy.

"Done!" said the other. "How long before he'll be ready?"

Sandy thought a moment.

"Another week," he said. "He won't have his weight before then. A week from to-day, we'll say. Next Tuesday night. Does that suit you, Harker?"

Harker nodded.

"Next Tuesday night," he agreed. Then he added, "I'll make it a *half* of my share that the Dane kills your wolf-dog."

Sandy took a long look at Kazan.

"I'll just take you on that," he said. Then, as he shook Harker's hand, "I don't believe there's a dog between here and the Yukon that can kill the wolf!"

XXIII

Professor McGill

Red Gold City was ripe for a night of relaxation. There had been some gambling, a few fights and enough liquor to create excitement now and then, but the presence of the mounted police had served to keep things unusually tame compared with events a few hundred miles farther north, in the Dawson country. The entertainment proposed by Sandy McTrigger and Jan Harker met with excited favor. The news spread for twenty miles about Red Gold City and there had never been greater excitement in the town than on the afternoon and night of the big fight. This was largely because Kazan and the huge Dane had been placed on exhibition, each dog in a specially made cage of his own, and a fever of betting began. Three hundred men, each of whom was paying five dollars to see the battle, viewed the gladiators through the bars of their cages. Harker's dog was a combination of Great Dane and mastiff, born in the North, and bred to the traces. Betting favored him by the odds of two to one. Occasionally it ran three to one. At these odds there was plenty of Kazan money. Those who were risking their money on him were the older wilderness men—men who had spent their lives among dogs, and who knew what the red glint in Kazan's eyes meant. An old Kootenay miner spoke low in another's ear:

"I'd bet on 'im even. I'd give odds if I had to. He'll fight all around the Dane. The Dane won't have no method."

"But he's got the weight," said the other dubiously. "Look at his jaws, an' his shoulders—"

"An' his big feet, an' his soft throat, an' the clumsy thickness of his belly," interrupted the Kootenay man. "For Gawd's sake, man, take my word for it, an' don't put your money on the Dane!"

Others thrust themselves between them. At first Kazan had snarled at all these faces about him. But now he lay back against the boarded side of the cage and eyed them sullenly from between his forepaws.

The fight was to be pulled off in Barker's place, a combination of saloon and cafe. The benches and tables had been cleared out and in the center of the one big room a cage ten feet square rested on a platform three and a half feet from the floor. Seats for the three hundred spectators were drawn closely around this. Suspended just above the open top of the cage were two big oil lamps with glass reflectors.

It was eight o'clock when Harker, McTrigger and two other men bore Kazan to the arena by means of the wooden bars that projected from the bottom of his cage. The big Dane was already in the fighting cage. He stood blinking his eyes in the brilliant light of the reflecting lamps. He pricked up his ears when he saw Kazan. Kazan did not show his fangs. Neither revealed the expected animosity. It was the first they had seen of each other, and a murmur of disappointment swept the ranks of the three hundred men. The Dane remained as motionless as a rock when Kazan was prodded from his own cage into the fighting cage. He did not leap or snarl. He regarded Kazan with a dubious questioning poise to his splendid head, and then looked again to the expectant and excited faces of the waiting men. For a few moments Kazan stood stiff-legged, facing the Dane. Then his shoulders dropped, and he, too, coolly faced the crowd that had expected a fight to the death. A laugh of derision swept through the closely seated rows. Catcalls, jeering taunts flung at McTrigger and Harker, and angry voices demanding their money back mingled with a tumult of growing discontent. Sandy's face was red with mortification and rage. The blue veins in Barker's forehead had swollen twice their normal size. He shook his fist in the face of the crowd, and shouted:

"Wait! Give 'em a chance, you dam' fools!"

At his words every voice was stilled. Kazan had turned. He was facing the huge Dane. And the Dane had turned his eyes to Kazan. Cautiously, prepared for a lunge or a sidestep, Kazan advanced a little. The Dane's shoulders bristled. He, too, advanced upon Kazan. Four feet apart they stood rigid. One could have heard a whisper in the room now. Sandy and Harker, standing close to the cage, scarcely breathed. Splendid in every limb and muscle, warriors of a hundred fights, and fearless to the point of death, the two half-wolf victims of man stood facing each other. None could see the questioning look in their brute eyes. None knew that in this thrilling moment the unseen hand of the wonderful Spirit God of the wilderness hovered between them, and that one of its miracles was descending upon them. It was *understanding*. Meeting in the open—rivals in the traces—they would have been rolling in the throes of terrific battle. But *here* came that mute appeal of brotherhood. In the final moment, when only a step separated them, and when men expected to see the first mad lunge, the splendid Dane slowly raised his head and looked over Kazan's back through the glare of the lights. Harker trembled, and under his breath he cursed. The Dane's throat was open to Kazan. But between the beasts had passed the voiceless pledge of peace. Kazan did not leap. He turned. And shoulder to shoulder—splendid in their contempt of man—they stood and looked through the bars of their prison into the one of human faces.

A roar burst from the crowd—a roar of anger, of demand, of threat. In his rage Harker drew a revolver and leveled it at the Dane. Above the tumult of the crowd a single voice stopped him.

"Hold!" it demanded. "Hold—in the name of the law!"

For a moment there was silence. Every face turned in the direction of the voice. Two men stood on chairs behind the last row. One was Sergeant Brokaw, of the Royal Northwest Mounted. It was he who had spoken. He was holding up a hand, commanding silence and attention. On the chair beside him stood another man. He was thin, with drooping shoulders, and a pale smooth face—a little man, whose physique and hollow cheeks told nothing of the years he had spent close up along the raw edge of the Arctic. It was he who spoke now, while the sergeant held up his hand. His voice was low and quiet:

"I'll give the owners five hundred dollars for those dogs," he said.

Every man in the room heard the offer. Harker looked at Sandy. For an instant their heads were close together.

"They won't fight, and they'll make good team-mates," the little man went on. "I'll give the owners five hundred dollars."

Harker raised a hand.

"Make it six," he said. "Make it six and they're yours."

The little man hesitated. Then he nodded.

"I'll give you six hundred," he agreed.

Murmurs of discontent rose throughout the crowd. Harker climbed to the edge of the platform.

"We ain't to blame because they wouldn't fight," he shouted, "but if there's any of you small enough to want your money back you can git it as you go out. The dogs laid down on us, that's all. We ain't to blame."

The little man was edging his way between the chairs, accompanied by the sergeant of police. With his pale face close to the sapling bars of the cage he looked at Kazan and the big Dane.

"I guess we'll be good friends," he said, and he spoke so low that only the dogs heard his voice. "It's a big price, but we'll charge it to the

JAMES OLIVER CURWOOD

Smithsonian, lads. I'm going to need a couple of four-footed friends of your moral caliber."

And no one knew why Kazan and the Dane drew nearer to the little scientist's side of the cage as he pulled out a big roll of bills and counted out six hundred dollars for Harker and Sandy McTrigger.

XXIV

Alone in Darkness

Never had the terror and loneliness of blindness fallen upon Gray Wolf as in the days that followed the shooting of Kazan and his capture by Sandy McTrigger. For hours after the shot she crouched in the bush back from the river, waiting for him to come to her. She had faith that he would come, as he had come a thousand times before, and she lay close on her belly, sniffing the air, and whining when it brought no scent of her mate. Day and night were alike an endless chaos of darkness to her now, but she knew when the sun went down. She sensed the first deepening shadows of evening, and she knew that the stars were out, and that the river lay in moonlight. It was a night to roam, and after a time she moved restlessly about in a small circle on the plain, and sent out her first inquiring call for Kazan. Up from the river came the pungent odor of smoke, and instinctively she knew that it was this smoke, and the nearness of man, that was keeping Kazan from her. But she went no nearer than that first circle made by her padded feet. Blindness had taught her to wait. Since the day of the battle on the Sun Rock, when the lynx had destroyed her eyes, Kazan had never failed her. Three times she called for him in the early night. Then she made herself a nest under a *banskian* shrub, and waited until dawn.

Just how she knew when night blotted out the last glow of the sun, so without seeing she knew when day came. Not until she felt the warmth of the sun on her back did her anxiety overcome her caution. Slowly she moved toward the river, sniffing the air and whining. There was no longer the smell of smoke in the air, and she could not catch the scent of man. She followed her own trail back to the sand-bar, and in the fringe of thick bush overhanging the white shore of the stream she stopped and listened. After a little she scrambled down and went straight to the spot where she and Kazan were drinking when the shot came. And there her nose struck the sand still wet and thick with Kazan's blood. She knew it was the blood of her mate, for the scent of him was all about her in the sand, mingled with the man-smell of Sandy McTrigger. She sniffed the trail of his body to the edge of the stream, where Sandy had dragged him to the canoe. She found the fallen tree to which he had been tied. And then she came upon one of the two clubs that Sandy had used to beat wounded Kazan into submissiveness. It was covered with blood and hair, and all at once Gray Wolf lay back on her haunches and turned her blind face to the sky, and there rose from her throat a cry for Kazan that drifted for miles on the wings of the south wind. Never had Gray Wolf given quite that cry before. It was not the "call" that comes with the moonlit nights, and neither was it the hunt-cry, nor the she-wolf's yearning for matehood. It carried with it the lament of death. And after that one cry Gray Wolf slunk back to the fringe of bush over the river, and lay with her face turned to the stream.

A strange terror fell upon her. She had grown accustomed to darkness, but never before had she been *alone* in that darkness. Always there had been the guardianship of Kazan's presence. She heard the clucking sound of a spruce hen in the bush a few yards away, and now that sound came to her as if from out of another world. A ground-mouse rustled through the grass close to her forepaws, and she snapped at it, and closed her teeth on a rock. The muscles of her shoulders twitched tremulously and she shivered as if stricken by intense cold. She was terrified by the darkness that shut out the world from her, and she pawed at her closed eyes, as if she might open them to light. Early in the afternoon she wandered back on the plain. It was different. It frightened her, and soon she returned to the beach, and snuggled down under the tree where Kazan had lain. She was not so frightened here. The smell of Kazan was strong about her. For an hour she lay motionless, with her head resting on the club clotted with his hair and blood. Night found her still there. And when the moon and the stars came out she crawled back into the pit in the white sand that Kazan's body had made under the tree.

With dawn she went down to the edge of the stream to drink. She could not see that the day was almost as dark as night, and that the gray-black sky was a chaos of slumbering storm. But she could smell the presence of it in the thick air, and could *feel* the forked flashes of lightning that rolled up with the dense pall from the south and west. The distant rumbling of thunder grew louder, and she huddled herself again under the tree. For hours the storm crashed over her, and the rain fell in a deluge. When it had finished she slunk out from her shelter like a thing beaten. Vainly she sought for one last scent of Kazan. The club was washed clean. Again the sand was white where Kazan's blood had reddened it. Even under the tree there was no sign of him left.

Until now only the terror of being alone in the pit of darkness that enveloped her had oppressed Gray Wolf. With afternoon came hunger. It was this hunger that drew her from the sand-bar, and she wandered back into the plain. A dozen times she scented game, and each time it evaded her. Even a ground-mouse that she cornered under a root, and dug out with her paws, escaped her fangs.

Thirty-six hours before this Kazan and Gray Wolf had left a half of their last kill a mile of two farther back on the plain. The kill was one of the big barren rabbits, and Gray Wolf turned in its direction. She did not require sight to find it. In her was developed to its finest point that sixth sense of the animal kingdom, the sense of orientation, and as straight as a pigeon might have winged its flight she cut through the bush to the spot where they had cached the rabbit. A white fox had been there ahead of her, and she found only scattered bits of hair and fur. What the fox had left the moose-birds and bush-jays had carried away. Hungrily Gray Wolf turned back to the river.

That night she slept again where Kazan had lain, and three times she called for him without answer. A heavy dew fell, and it drenched the last vestige of her mate's scent out of the sand. But still through the day that followed, and the day that followed that, blind Gray Wolf clung to the narrow rim of white sand. On the fourth day her hunger reached a point where she gnawed the bark from willow bushes. It was on this day that she made a discovery. She was drinking, when her sensitive nose touched something in the water's edge that was smooth, and bore a faint odor of flesh. It was one of the big northern river clams. She pawed it ashore, sniffing at the hard shell. Then she crunched it between her teeth. She had never tasted sweeter meat than that which she found inside, and she began hunting for other clams. She found many of them, and ate until she was no longer hungry. For three days more she remained on the bar.

And then, one night, the call came to her. It set her quivering with a strange new excitement—something that may have been a new hope, and in the moonlight she trotted nervously up and down the shining strip of sand, facing now the north, and now the south, and then the east and the west—her head flung up, listening, as if in the soft wind of the night she was trying to locate the whispering lure of a wonderful voice. And whatever it was that came to her came from out of the south and east. Off there—across the barren, far beyond the outer edge of the northern timber-line—was *home*. And off there, in her brute way, she reasoned that she must find Kazan. The call did not come from their old windfall home in the swamp. It came from beyond that, and in a flashing vision there rose through her blindness a picture of the towering Sun Rock, of the winding trail that led to it, and the cabin on the plain. It was there that blindness had come to her. It was there that day had ended, and eternal night had begun. And it was there that she had mothered her first-born. Nature had registered these things so that they could never be wiped out of her memory, and when the call came it was from the sunlit world where she had last known light and life and had last seen the moon and the stars in the blue night of the skies.

And to that call she responded, leaving the river and its food behind her—straight out into the face of darkness and starvation, no longer fearing death or the emptiness of the world she could not see; for ahead of her, two hundred miles away, she could see the Sun Rock, the winding trail, the nest of her first-born between the two big rocks—*and Kazan*!

XXV

THE LAST OF MCTRIGGER

Sixty miles farther north Kazan lay at the end of his fine steel chain, watching little Professor McGill mixing a pail of tallow and bran. A dozen yards from him lay the big Dane, his huge jaws drooling in anticipation of the unusual feast which McGill was preparing. He showed signs of pleasure when McGill approached him with a quart of the mixture, and he gulped it between his huge jaws. The little man with the cold blue eyes and the gray-blond hair stroked his back without fear. His attitude was different when he turned to Kazan. His movements were filled with caution, and yet his eyes and his lips were smiling, and he gave the wolf-dog no evidence of his fear, if it could be called fear.

The little professor, who was up in the north country for the Smithsonian Institution, had spent a third of his life among dogs. He loved them, and understood them. He had written a number of magazine articles on dog intellect that had attracted wide attention among naturalists. It was largely because he loved dogs, and understood them more than most men, that he had bought Kazan and the big Dane on the night when Sandy McTrigger and his partner had tried to get them to fight to the death in the Red Gold City saloon. The refusal of the two splendid beasts to kill each other for the pleasure of the three hundred men who had assembled to witness the fight delighted him. He had already planned a paper on the incident. Sandy had told him the story of Kazan's capture, and of his wild mate, Gray Wolf, and the professor had asked him a thousand questions. But each day Kazan puzzled him more. No amount of kindness on his part could bring a responsive gleam in Kazan's eyes. Not once did Kazan signify a willingness to become friends. And yet he did not snarl at McGill, or snap at his hands when they came within reach. Quite frequently Sandy McTrigger came over to the little cabin where McGill was staying, and three times Kazan leaped at the end of his chain to get at him, and his white fangs gleamed as long as Sandy was in sight. Alone with McGill he became quiet. Something told him that McGill had come as a friend that night when he and the big Dane stood shoulder to shoulder in the cage that had been built for a slaughter pen. Away down in his brute heart he held McGill apart from other men. He had no desire to harm him. He tolerated him, but showed none of the growing affection of the huge Dane. It was this fact that puzzled McGill. He had never before known a dog that he could not make love him.

To-day he placed the tallow and bran before Kazan, and the smile in his face gave way to a look of perplexity. Kazan's lips had drawn suddenly back. A fierce snarl rolled deep in his throat. The hair along his spine stood up. His muscles twitched. Instinctively the professor turned. Sandy McTrigger had come up quietly behind him. His brutal face wore a grin as he looked at Kazan.

"It's a fool job—tryin' to make friends with *him*" he said. Then he added, with a sudden interested gleam in his eyes, "When you startin'?"

"With first frost," replied McGill. "It ought to come soon. I'm going to join Sergeant Conroy and his party at Fond du Lac by the first of October."

"And you're going up to Fond du Lac—alone?" queried Sandy. "Why don't you take a man?"

The little professor laughed softly.

"Why?" he asked. "I've been through the Athabasca waterways a dozen times, and know the trail as well as I know Broadway. Besides, I like to be alone. And the work isn't too hard, with the currents all flowing to the north and east."

Sandy was looking at the Dane, with his back to McGill. An exultant gleam shot for an instant into his eyes.

"You're taking the dogs?"

"Yes."

Sandy lighted his pipe, and spoke like one strangely curious.

"Must cost a heap to take these trips o' yourn, don't it?"

"My last cost about seven thousand dollars. This will cost five," said McGill.

"Gawd!" breathed Sandy. "An' you carry all that along with you! Ain't you afraid—something might happen—?"

The little professor was looking the other way now. The carelessness in his face and manner changed. His blue eyes grew a shade darker. A hard smile which Sandy did not see hovered about his lips for an instant. Then he turned, laughing.

"I'm a very light sleeper," he said. "A footstep at night rouses me. Even a man's breathing awakes me, when I make up my mind that I must be on my guard. And, besides"—he drew from his pocket a blue-steeled

Savage automatic—"I know how to use *this*." He pointed to a knot in the wall of the cabin. "Observe," he said. Five times he fired at twenty paces, and when Sandy went up to look at the knot he gave a gasp. There was one jagged hole where the knot had been.

"Pretty good," he grinned. "Most men couldn't do better'n that with a rifle."

When Sandy left, McGill followed him with a suspicious gleam in his eyes, and a curious smile on his lips. Then he turned to Kazan.

"Guess you've got him figgered out about right, old man," he laughed softly. "I don't blame you very much for wanting to get him by the throat. Perhaps—"

He shoved his hands deep in his pockets, and went into the cabin. Kazan dropped his head between his forepaws, and lay still, with wide-open eyes. It was late afternoon, early in September, and each night brought now the first chill breaths of autumn. Kazan watched the last glow of the sun as it faded out of the southern skies. Darkness always followed swiftly after that, and with darkness came more fiercely his wild longing for freedom. Night after night he had gnawed at his steel chain. Night after night he had watched the stars, and the moon, and had listened for Gray Wolf's call, while the big Dane lay sleeping. Tonight it was colder than usual, and the keen tang of the wind that came fresh from the west stirred him strangely. It set his blood afire with what the Indians call the Frost Hunger. Lethargic summer was gone and the days and nights of hunting were at hand. He wanted to leap out into freedom and run until he was exhausted, with Gray Wolf at his side. He knew that Gray Wolf was off there—where the stars hung low in the clear sky, and that she was waiting. He strained at the end of his chain, and whined. All that night he was restless—more restless than he had been at any time before. Once, in the far distance, he heard a cry that he thought was the cry of Gray Wolf, and his answer roused McGill from deep sleep. It was dawn, and the little professor dressed himself and came out of the cabin. With satisfaction he noted the exhilarating snap in the air. He wet his fingers and held them above his head, chuckling when he found the wind had swung into the north. He went to Kazan, and talked to him. Among other things he said, "This'll put the black flies to sleep, Kazan. A day or two more of it and we'll start."

Five days later McGill led first the Dane, and then Kazan, to a packed canoe. Sandy McTrigger saw them off, and Kazan watched for a chance to leap at him. Sandy kept his distance, and McGill watched the two with a thought that set the blood running swiftly behind the mask of his careless smile. They had slipped a mile down-stream when he leaned over and laid a fearless hand on Kazan's head. Something in the touch of that hand, and in the professor's voice, kept Kazan from a desire to snap at him. He tolerated the friendship with expressionless eyes and a motionless body.

"I was beginning to fear I wouldn't have much sleep, old boy," chuckled McGill ambiguously, "but I guess I can take a nap now and then with *you* along!"

He made camp that night fifteen miles up the lake shore. The big Dane he fastened to a sapling twenty yards from his small silk tent, but Kazan's chain he made fast to the butt of a stunted birch that held down the tent-flap. Before he went into the tent for the night McGill pulled out his automatic and examined it with care.

For three days the journey continued without a mishap along the shore of Lake Athabasca. On the fourth night McGill pitched his tent in a clump of *banskian* pine a hundred yards back from the water. All that day the wind had come steadily from behind them, and for at least a half of the day the professor had been watching Kazan closely. From the west there had now and then come a scent that stirred him uneasily. Since noon he had sniffed that wind. Twice McGill had heard him growling deep in his throat, and once, when the scent had come stronger than usual, he had bared his fangs, and the bristles stood up along his spine. For an hour after striking camp the little professor did not build a fire, but sat looking up the shore of the lake through his hunting glass. It was dusk when he returned to where he had put up his tent and chained the dogs. For a few moments he stood unobserved, looking at the wolf-dog. Kazan was still uneasy. He lay *facing* the west. McGill made note of this, for the big Dane lay behind Kazan—to the east. Under ordinary conditions Kazan would have faced him. He was sure now that there was something in the west wind. A little shiver ran up his back as he thought of what it might be.

Behind a rock he built a very small fire, and prepared supper. After this he went into the tent, and when he came out he carried a blanket under his arm. He chuckled as he stood for a moment over Kazan.

"We're not going to sleep in there to-night, old hoy," he said. "I don't like what you've found in the west wind. It may he a—*thunder-storm!*" He laughed at his joke, and buried himself in a clump of stunted *banskians* thirty paces from the tent. Here he rolled himself in his blanket, and went to sleep.

It was a quiet starlit night, and hours afterward Kazan dropped his nose between his forepaws and drowsed. It was the snap of a twig that roused him. The sound did not awaken the sluggish Dane but instantly Kazan's head was alert, his keen nostrils sniffing the air. What he had smelled all day was heavy about him now. He lay still and quivering. Slowly, from out of the *banskians* behind the tent, there came a figure. It was not the little professor. It approached cautiously, with lowered head and hunched shoulders, and the starlight revealed the murderous face of Sandy McTrigger. Kazan crouched low. He laid his head flat between his forepaws. His long fangs gleamed. But he made no sound that betrayed his concealment under a thick *banskian* shrub. Step by step Sandy approached, and at last he reached the flap of the tent. He did not carry a club or a whip in his hand now. In the place of either of those was the glitter of steel. At the door to the tent he paused, and peered in, his back to Kazan.

Silently, swiftly—the wolf now in every movement, Kazan came to his feet. He forgot the chain that held him. Ten feet away stood the enemy he hated above all others he had ever known. Every ounce of strength in his splendid body gathered itself for the spring. And then he leaped. This time the chain did not pull him back, almost neck-broken. Age and the elements had weakened the leather collar he had worn since the days of his slavery in the traces, and it gave way with a snap. Sandy turned, and in a second leap Kazan's fangs sank into the flesh of his arm. With a startled cry the man fell, and as they rolled over on the ground the big Dane's deep voice rolled out in thunderous alarm as he tugged at his leash. In the fall Kazan's hold was broken. In an instant he was on his feet, ready for another attack. And then the change came. He was *free*. The collar was gone from his neck. The forest, the stars, the whispering wind were all about him. *Here* were men, and off there was—Gray Wolf! His ears dropped, and he turned swiftly, and slipped like a shadow back into the glorious freedom of his world.

A hundred yards away something stopped him for an instant. It was not the big Dane's voice, but the sharp *crack—crack—crack*, of the little professor's automatic. And above that sound there rose the voice of Sandy McTrigger in a weird and terrible cry.

XXVI

An Empty World

Mile after mile Kazan went on. For a time he was oppressed by the shivering note of death that had come to him in Sandy McTrigger's cry, and he slipped through the *banskians* like a shadow, his ears flattened, his tail trailing, his hindquarters betraying that curious slinking quality of the wolf and dog stealing away from danger. Then he came out upon a plain, and the stillness, the billion stars in the clear vault of the sky, and the keen air that carried with it a breath of the Arctic barrens made him alert and questioning. He faced the direction of the wind. Somewhere off there, far to the south and west, was Gray Wolf. For the first time in many weeks he sat back on his haunches and gave the deep and vibrant call that echoed weirdly for miles about him. Back in the *banskians* the big Dane heard it, and whined. From over the still body of Sandy McTrigger the little professor looked up with a white tense face, and listened for a second cry. But instinct told Kazan that to that first call there would be no answer, and now he struck out swiftly, galloping mile after mile, as a dog follows the trail of its master home. He did not turn back to the lake, nor was his direction toward Red Gold City. As straight as he might have followed a road blazed by the hand of man he cut across the forty miles of plain and swamp and forest and rocky ridge that lay between him and the McFarlane. All that night he did not call again for Gray Wolf. With him reasoning was a process brought about by habit—by precedent—and as Gray Wolf had waited for him many times before he knew that she would be waiting for him now near the sand-bar.

By dawn he had reached the river, within three miles of the sand-bar. Scarcely was the sun up when he stood on the white strip of sand where he and Gray Wolf had come down to drink. Expectantly and confidently he looked about him for Gray Wolf, whining softly, and wagging his tail. He began to search for her scent, but rains had washed even her footprints from the clean sand. All that day he searched for her along the river and out on the plain. He went to where they had killed their last rabbit. He sniffed at the bushes where the poison baits had hung. Again and again he sat back on his haunches and sent out his mating cry to her. And slowly, as he did these things, nature was working in him that miracle of the wild which the Crees have named the "spirit call." As it had worked in Gray Wolf, so now it stirred the blood of Kazan. With the going of the sun, and the sweeping about him of shadowy night, he turned more and more to the south and east. His whole world was made up of the trails over which he had hunted. Beyond those places he did not know that there was such a thing as existence. And in that world, small in his understanding of things, was Gray Wolf. He could not miss her. That world, in his comprehension of it, ran from the McFarlane in a narrow trail through the forests and over the plains to the little valley from which the beavers had driven them. If Gray Wolf was not here—she was there, and tirelessly he resumed his quest of her.

Not until the stars were fading out of the sky again, and gray day was giving place to night, did exhaustion and hunger stop him. He killed a rabbit, and for hours after he had feasted he lay close to his kill, and slept. Then he went on.

The fourth night he came to the little valley between the two ridges, and under the stars, more brilliant now in the chill clearness of the early autumn nights, he followed the creek down into their old swamp home. It was broad day when he reached the edge of the great beaver pond that now completely surrounded the windfall under which Gray-Wolf's second-born had come into the world. Broken Tooth and the other beavers had wrought a big change in what had once been his home and Gray Wolf's, and for many minutes Kazan stood silent and motionless at the edge of the pond, sniffing the air heavy with the unpleasant odor of the usurpers. Until now his spirit had remained unbroken. Footsore, with thinned sides and gaunt head, he circled slowly through the swamp. All that day he searched. And his crest lay flat now, and there was a hunted look in the droop of his shoulders and in the shifting look of his eyes. Gray Wolf was gone.

Slowly nature was impinging that fact upon him. She had passed out of his world and out of his life, and he was filled with a loneliness and a grief so great that the forest seemed strange, and the stillness of the wild a thing that now oppressed and frightened him. Once more the dog in him was mastering the wolf. With Gray Wolf he had possessed the world of freedom. Without her, that world was so big and strange and empty that it appalled him. Late in the afternoon he came upon a little pile of crushed clamshells on the shore of the stream. He sniffed at them—turned away—went back, and sniffed again. It was where Gray

Wolf had made a last feast in the swamp before continuing south. B
the scent she had left behind was not strong enough to tell Kazan, an
for a second time he turned away. That night he slunk under a log, and
cried himself to sleep. Deep in the night he grieved in his uneasy slumber,
like a child. And day after day, and night after night, Kazan remained a
slinking creature of the big swamp, mourning for the one creature that
had brought him out of chaos into light, who had filled his world for
him, and who, in going from him, had taken from this world even the
things that Gray Wolf had lost in her blindness.

XXVII

The Call of Sun Rock

In the golden glow of the autumn sun there came up the stream overlooked by the Sun Rock one day a man, a woman and a child in a canoe. Civilization had done for lovely Joan what it had done for many another wild flower transplanted from the depths of the wilderness. Her cheeks were thin. Her blue eyes had lost their luster. She coughed, and when she coughed the man looked at her with love and fear in his eyes. But now, slowly, the man had begun to see the transformation, and on the day their canoe pointed up the stream and into the wonderful valley that had been their home before the call of the distant city came to them, he noted the flush gathering once more in her cheeks, the fuller redness of her lips, and the gathering glow of happiness and content in her eyes. He laughed softly as he saw these things, and he blessed the forests. In the canoe she had leaned back, with her head almost against his shoulder, and he stopped paddling to draw her to him, and run his fingers through the soft golden masses of her hair.

"You are happy again, Joan," he laughed joyously. "The doctors were right. You are a part of the forests."

"Yes, I am happy," she whispered, and suddenly there came a little thrill into her voice, and she pointed to a white finger of sand running out into the stream. "Do you remember—years and years ago, it seems—that Kazan left us here? *She* was on the sand over there, calling to him. Do you remember?" There was a little tremble about her mouth, and she added, "I wonder—where they—have gone."

The cabin was as they had left it. Only the crimson *bakneesh* had grown up about it, and shrubs and tall grass had sprung up near its walls. Once more it took on life, and day by day the color came deeper into Joan's cheeks, and her voice was filled with its old wild sweetness of song. Joan's husband cleared the trails over his old trap-lines, and Joan and the little Joan, who romped and talked now, transformed the cabin into *home*. One night the man returned to the cabin late, and when he came in there was a glow of excitement in Joan's blue eyes, and a tremble in her voice when she greeted him.

"Did you hear it?" she asked. "Did you hear—*the call*?"

He nodded, stroking her soft hair.

"I was a mile back in the creek swamp," he said. "I heard it!"

Joan's hands clutched his arms.

"It wasn't Kazan," she said. "I would recognize *his* voice. But it seemed to me it was like the other—the call that came that morning from the sand-bar, his *mate*?"

The man was thinking. Joan's fingers tightened. She was breathing a little quickly.

"Will you promise me this?" she asked, "Will you promise me that you will never hunt or trap for wolves?"

"I had thought of that," he replied. "I thought of it—after I heard the call. Yes, I will promise."

Joan's arms stole up about his neck.

"We loved Kazan," she whispered. "And you might kill him—or *her*"

Suddenly she stopped. Both listened. The door was a little ajar, and to them there came again the wailing mate-call of the wolf. Joan ran to the door. Her husband followed. Together they stood silent, and with tense breath Joan pointed over the starlit plain.

"Listen! Listen!" she commanded. "It's her cry, *and it came from the Sun Rock*!"

She ran out into the night, forgetting that the man was close behind her now, forgetting that little Joan was alone in her bed. And to them, from miles and miles across the plain, there came a wailing cry in answer—a cry that seemed a part of the wind, and that thrilled Joan until her breath broke in a strange sob.

Farther out on the plain she went and then stopped, with the golden glow of the autumn moon and the stars shimmering in her hair and eyes. It was many minutes before the cry came again, and then it was so near that Joan put her hands to her mouth, and her cry rang out over the plain as in the days of old.

"*Kazan! Kazan! Kazan!*"

At the top of the Sun Rock, Gray Wolf—gaunt and thinned by starvation—heard the woman's cry, and the call that was in her throat died away in a whine. And to the north a swiftly moving shadow stopped for a moment, and stood like a thing of rock under the starlight. It was Kazan. A strange fire leaped through his body. Every fiber of his brute understanding was afire with the knowledge that here was *home*.

It was here, long ago, that he had lived, and loved, and fought—and all at once the dreams that had grown faded and indistinct in his memory came back to him as real living things. For, coming to him faintly over the plain, *he heard Joan's voice!*

In the starlight Joan stood, tense and white, when from out of the pale mists of the moon-glow he came to her, cringing on his belly, panting and wind-run, and with a strange whining note in his throat. And as Joan went to him, her arms reaching out, her lips sobbing his name over and over again, the man stood and looked down upon them with the wonder of a new and greater understanding in his face. He had no fear of the wolf-dog now. And as Joan's arms hugged Kazan's great shaggy head up to her he heard the whining gasping joy of the beast and the sobbing whispering voice of the girl, and with tensely gripped hands he faced the Sun Rock.

"My Gawd," he breathed. "I believe—it's so—"

As if in response to the thought in his mind, there came once more across the plain Gray Wolf's mate-seeking cry of grief and of loneliness. Swiftly as though struck by a lash Kazan was on his feet—oblivious of Joan's touch, of her voice, of the presence of the man. In another instant he was gone, and Joan flung herself against her husband's breast, and almost fiercely took his face between her two hands.

"*Now* do you believe?" she cried pantingly. "*Now* do you believe in the God of my world—the God I have lived with, the God that gives souls to the wild things, the God that—that has brought—us, all—together—once more—*home!*"

His arms closed gently about her.

"I believe, my Joan," he whispered.

"And you understand—now—what it means, 'Thou shalt not kill'?"

"Except that it brings us life—yes, I understand," he replied.

Her warm soft hands stroked his face. Her blue eyes, filled with the glory of the stars, looked up into his.

"Kazan and *she*—you and I—and the baby! Are you sorry—that we came back?" she asked.

So close he drew her against his breast that she did not hear the words he whispered in the soft warmth of her hair. And after that, for many hours, they sat in the starlight in front of the cabin door. But they did not hear again that lonely cry from the Sun Rock. Joan and her husband understood.

"He'll visit us again to-morrow," the man said at last. "Come, Joan, let us go to bed."

Together they entered the cabin.

And that night, side by side, Kazan and Gray Wolf hunted again in the moonlit plain.

A Note About the Author

James Oliver Curwood (1878–1927) was an American writer and conservationist popular in the action-adventure genre. Curwood began his career as a journalist, and was hired by the Canadian government to travel around Northern Canada and publish travel journals in order to encourage tourism. This served as a catalyst for his works of fiction, which were often set in Alaska or the Hudson Bay area in Canada. Curwood was among the top ten best-selling authors in the United States during the early and mid 1920s. Over one-hundred and eighty films have been inspired by or based on his work. With these deals paired with his record book sales, Curwood earned an impressive amount of wealth from his work. As he grew older, Curwood became an advocate for conservationism and environmentalism, giving up his hunting hobby and serving on conservation committees. Between his activism and his literary work, Curwood helped shape the popular perception of the natural world.

A Note from the Publisher

Spanning many genres, from non-fiction essays to literature classics to children's books and lyric poetry, Mint Edition books showcase the master works of our time in a modern new package. The text is freshly typeset, is clean and easy to read, and features a new note about the author in each volume. Many books also include exclusive new introductory material. Every book boasts a striking new cover, which makes it as appropriate for collecting as it is for gift giving. Mint Edition books are only printed when a reader orders them, so natural resources are not wasted. We're proud that our books are never manufactured in excess and exist only in the exact quantity they need to be read and enjoyed.

Discover more of your favorite classics with Bookfinity™.

- Track your reading with custom book lists.
- Get great book recommendations for your personalized Reader Type.
- Add reviews for your favorite books.
- AND MUCH MORE!

Visit **bookfinity.com** and take the fun Reader Type quiz to get started.

Enjoy our classic and modern companion pairings!

Printed in the USA
CPSIA information can be obtained
at www.ICGtesting.com
JSHW082344140824
68134JS00020B/1867

9 781513 280738